By Louis Begley
Published by The Random House Publishing Group

WARTIME LIES
THE MAN WHO WAS LATE
AS MAX SAW IT
ABOUT SCHMIDT
MISTLER'S EXIT
SCHMIDT DELIVERED

WARTIME LIES

Louis Begley

BALLANTINE BOOKS • NEW YORK

A Ballantine Book
Published by The Random House Publishing Group
Copyright © 1991 by Louis Begley

All rights reserved under International and Pan-American Copyright Conventions. Published in the United States by The Random House Publishing Group, a division of Random House, Inc., New York, and simultaneously in Canada by Random House of Canada Limited, Toronto.

Ballantine and colophon are registered trademarks of Random House, Inc.

www.ballantinebooks.com

Library of Congress Catalog Card Number: 90-53429

ISBN 0-8041-0990-7

This edition published by arrangement with Alfred A. Knopf, Inc.

Printed in Canada

First Ballantine Books: July 1992

21   20   19   18   17   16   15

For my mother

TAKE A MAN WITH A NICE FACE AND SAD EYES, FIFTY or more winters on his back, living a moderately pleasant life in a tranquil country. He is a bookish fellow, the sort you would expect to find in a good publishing house or at a local university teaching how to compare one literature with another. He might even be a literary agent with a flair for dissident writing: texts bearing witness against oppression and inhumanity. Sometimes, in the evening, he reads Latin classics. There is no question anymore of his being able to do a version. He learned Latin in great globs to pass whatever examination happened to be blocking his path, always in the very nick of time; his knowledge was never precise. Fortunately, the power to grasp meaning and to remember has remained. He reveres the Aeneid. That is where he first found civil expression for his own shame at being alive, his skin intact and virgin of tattoo, when his kinsmen and almost all the others, so many surely more deserving than he, perished in the conflagration.

He takes care to keep the metaphor at a distance. His native town in eastern Poland was no Ilium, and even if some SS blackshirt, imperturbably beating an aged former human being with a riding crop, is a pretty good stand-in for Pyrrhus slaughtering Priam, where, in that senseless tableau, are the contending golden-haired gods and goddesses? He has seen such a beating, administered to a totally bald man forced to kneel, the blows aimed at the top of the head, the man's hands folded behind his back, unable to wipe the blood streaming down his face. What insult to what goddess was avenged by that outrage? Did Jove, sulking, order into action the detail of old Jews so usefully engaged in cleaning street gutters, also on their knees, under the supervision of Jewish militiamen, long staves held at the ready?

Now he caresses the metaphors. When Aeneas plays the tourist in Carthage, thoughtfully enveloped in a cloud by his immortal mother, his astonished eyes behold scenes of Trojan slaughter portrayed artfully on Dido's palace walls. Did not our man himself, quickly after his war ended, see in the first books of photographs of Auschwitz, Bergen-Belsen and Buchenwald naked, skeletal men and women alive and staring at the camera, corpses lying in disorderly piles, warehouses of eyeglasses, watches and shoes? Where is the sense of his survival? Father Aeneas fleeing Troy with little Iulus fulfills an immutable promise: he will found eternal Rome; by the will of Jove and a twist of the tongue, Ascanius-Iulus will become the forebear of the Julian Caesars. Our man, sea-tossed, hollowed out and bereft, thinks he has no discernible destiny. His memorable scenes are the stuff of nightmares, not myth.

Our man avoids Holocaust books and dinner conversations about Poland in the Second World War even if his neighbor is beautiful, her eyes promising perfumed consolation. Yet he pores over accounts of the torture of dissidents and political prisoners, imagining minutely each session. How long would it have been before he cried and groveled? Right away, or only after they had broken his fingers? Whom would he have betrayed and

*how quickly? He has become a voyeur of evil, some-
times uncertain which role he plays in the vile pictures
that pass before his eyes. Is that the inevitable evolution
of the child he once was, the price to be paid for his
sort of survival?*

*A different affinity draws him to Catullus, a beacon
flashing across black water. He imagines the poet's
childhood near Verona, the charming Sabine villa,
the swift yacht. A tender father accompanies Catullus to Rome and sees to his establishment there. The
poet loves Lesbia, beautiful nymphomaniac Lesbia,
loves her not as the common run of men love a girl
but as a Roman loves his sons and sons-in-law. Alas,
love for Lesbia is a sickness. Lesbia, whom Catullus
loves more than himself and all his tribe, turns tricks
in doorways and alleys. The poet no longer wishes
her to be faithful, even if that were possible. He
wants to heal, to be well, to throw off the foul sickness that has robbed him of his enjoyments.* Ipse val-
ere opto et taetrum hunc deponere morbum. . . . *The
lines have haunted our man for years, he thinks he
knows Catullus's sickness to the bone, he too has
wanted to heal and to be well regardless of all else.
Only this metaphor, too, fails. His disease lies deeper
than the poet's. Catullus never doubts he was born
to be happy and to have pleasure in past good deeds,*
benefacta priora voluptas. *The gods owe him as much
for his piety.* O di, reddite mi hoc pro pietate mea.
*The man with sad eyes believes he has been changed
inside forever, like a beaten dog, and gods will not
cure that. He has no good deeds to look back upon.
Still, it is better to say the poem over and over. He
will not howl over his own despair.*

He thinks on the story of the child that became such

a man. For the sake of an old song, he calls the child Maciek: polite little Maciek, dancing tirelessly while the music plays.

I

I WAS BORN A FEW MONTHS AFTER THE BURNING OF the Reichstag in T., a town of about forty thousand in a part of Poland that before the Great War had belonged to the Austro-Hungarian Empire. My father was T.'s leading physician. Neither the Catholic surgeon who was the director of the hospital nor my father's two general practitioner colleagues had his Viennese university diplomas, his reputation as a *Zeller* marked for academic success—already acquired in the first year of the *gimnazjum* and confirmed when he received one of the gold watches the Emperor Franz Josef reserved each year for the most brilliant graduating students in the realm—or, for that matter, his overflowing kindness and devotion to patients. My mother, a beauty from Cracow who was much younger than he, died in childbirth. The marriage had been arranged by a matchmaker, but the doctor and the beauty fell in love with a rapidity that became a family fable, and my father swore that he would devote what remained of his life to my mother's memory and to me. For a very long time he kept his word.

My mother's older sister, even more beautiful and, now that she was the only child, much richer, was by common consent unlikely ever to marry—not even her widowed brother-in-law. In the closed world of wealthy Galician Jews, she was haunted by indistinct tales of a romance with a Catholic painter, a missed elopement,

5

and a suspicion that the artist's subsequent actions were strongly influenced first by the vision of her dowry, and then by the vision's disappearance in the wake of my grandfather's rage, directed with equal force at the religion and bohemianism of my aunt's friend. With other women, such things might have been conveniently forgotten by more acceptable amateurs of good looks and money and their mothers and other female relations on the lookout for brides. But Tania, for that was my aunt's name, could hope for no such indulgence. She was known as widely for her irreverence and implacably sharp tongue as for her stubbornness and bad temper. It was said that she was a female version of her father: a man whom anyone would want as a business partner but no thoughtful and well-informed person would have seriously considered acquiring as a husband or a son-in-law.

Besides, there was the shadow—family bad luck or bad blood—cast over both my mother and Tania by the suicide, some years earlier, of their younger brother. Refused admission to the university (this was at the beginning of the imposition of Jewish quotas in Poland), in love with a girl whose application had been accepted, he took to spending the days of the summer vacation on horseback, wandering through the forest that bordered my grandfather's property. On one of his expeditions, he was surprised by a violent thunderstorm. He dismounted, took refuge under a tree, and, holding his horse by the reins, tried to calm him by stroking and kissing his nostrils. Lightning struck very close. The horse panicked and bit my uncle repeatedly on the face. The scars were very ugly. The girl seemed more distant; my uncle didn't know whether to blame distractions of university life or revulsion. Which reason was worse? Efforts were made to find a place for him in a university abroad, but before the fall semester was over, he went one afternoon to the stable and killed his horse and himself with two rounds of shot.

So it happened that Tania came to live with us, to make a home for my father and to bring me up.

We continued to occupy the house where I was born, bought with my mother's dowry directly after the marriage. The house stood in a garden on the principal street of T. Our family quarters and my father's office filled the one-story wing that ran parallel to the street. In the other wing, at a right angle with ours, with its entrance in the courtyard, a *gimnazjum* teacher and his wife lived on the ground floor; the second-floor tenants were a stationery store owner, Pan Kramer, his wife, and their daughter Irena, who was two or three years older than I. Until the Germans came, Irena and I never played together: my father did not think it proper.

Like every male in Poland old enough to shave, father Kramer was addressed as Pan; only servants, peasants and manual laborers were denied that honorific syllable. Mother Kramer was Pani Kramerowa or Pani Renata to all but her family and intimate friends. Irena should in time have been known as Panna Kramerówna or Panna Irena or, because the Polish language loves diminutives for food, drink and names, Panna Irka.

Our living room was separated from my father's study, where he received patients after their turn in the examination room, by a wide, padded, white door. Adjacent to the door was a huge white porcelain stove. Sometimes in the night, through that door or through the space between the stove and the wall, where kindling and some of my toys were stored, emerged the square-shouldered white giant of my nightmares. It served no purpose when my nurse opened the door and carried me, screaming and rigid, into the familiar ter-

rain of my father's study, or laid out on the rug in front
of the stove one by one each piece of kindling and each
little truck or shovel so that I could see that nothing,
nothing at all, let alone a giant, could have hidden behind them. My terror only increased along with my
screams, and soon it would be necessary to send a horse
cab to fetch Tania or my father from the restaurant or
café where they might be.

At that time, when my memories of the monster and
the other circumstances of my life begin to be my own,
rather than stories of that idyllic time that Tania later
told me during the war years, she and my father were
out most evenings. My father finished his house calls
early. He would then play with me until it was time to
meet the two married Jewish doctors and their wives
for dinner or for coffee. The café, understood as a Viennese institution, thrived in T. It was never too soon
or too late to find a friend there. One lingered, or perhaps went to another café or a restaurant where there
was dancing. Tania sometimes accompanied my father.
More frequently, she joined Bern, the richest Jewish
lawyer in T. and an acknowledged old bachelor. In contrast to my father, Bern was a bon vivant, proud of his
legendary ability to absorb Tokay and vodka. He was
also an expert dancer. To coax me out of my dread at
the prospect of her going out, Tania would sometimes
have him wind up the gramophone when he came to
call for her, and they would rehearse his specialties: the
slow waltz and the tango.

In the summer, after his nap, my father met Bern,
the Catholic surgeon, and one or the other of his Jewish
doctor friends for tennis. Tania often took me to watch
these matches. On other afternoons, we would go to the
beach—a strip of riverbank painstakingly covered each
season with a thick layer of white sand. An entrance

fee made the beach exclusive and entitled those who paid to the comfort of deck chairs, parasols and changing cabins. Only the more intrepid swimmers braved the river's swift currents, using a leisurely, face-out-of-water style of breaststroke. Men and women alike wore white rubber bonnets. Some finicky bathers, my father among them, also put on white rubber shoes like ballet slippers to protect their feet from pebbles and the slimy feel of the bottom. By the time I was four, Tania and my father took turns teaching me how to swim. To their relief, I was an eager pupil.

Much as Tania tried to protect my reputation, it was understood in T. that I was a difficult, troubling child. The wet nurse remained with us for the first year after my mother died—to keep her longer was against Tania's principles and, probably, my father's as well—but it was discovered soon after her departure that I didn't want to eat. Mealtimes turned into tests of will between Tania and me, with the cook, the maid, the current nurse and, at moments of great crisis, even the laundress in attendance. Tania usually won. I took my revenge later by vomiting whatever combination of delicacies and essential sources of iron and vitamins I had been made to ingest. The chamber pot also tested her resolution and mine. Like all nicely brought up children of that era, I had been toilet trained very early, and I took the training to heart. By the time I was three, getting me to excrete was an elaborate process, involving installing the pot in the middle of the kitchen, sitting me on it, and pleading and threatening, with the same group that witnessed my defeats in the struggle against intake assembled to see the output. Tania had a repertoire of helpful incantations. Quickly now, one-two-three, we're all waiting here to see. Make, Maciek, make. If encouragement failed, an enema would be administered. I loathed my own smell.

A cardiologist specializing in children heard an irregularity in my heartbeat. Another specialist confirmed it. A third disagreed. My father could not hear the offending noise himself but thought it wrong to disregard the views of two eminent professors. It was obvious to all that I was scrawny and nervous. The nightmare of the giant recurred with increasing frequency. I filled the house with shrieks. No nurse proved equal for more than a few months to contending with both Tania and me during the day and then with me at night. These nurses all were called Panny, spectacle-wearing young ladies, daughters of impecunious but relatively assimilated Jewish families, earning their way to a place of higher learning. Tania would give them scarves and hats and advise them on makeup and permanent waves that would bring out the best in their looks and yet were suitably modest. She scolded them about runs in their stockings and corrected them at the piano. Mousy, high-strung, these young women were good at reading to me and teaching me to read. They were grateful to Tania, pitied her (such an extraordinary person wasting her life in T. out of love for her family!), and left with letters of reference from my father.

Then Zosia arrived, on the recommendation of the Catholic surgeon. He had lanced a boil on my thigh and returned several times to rebandage the wound. What Maciek needs, he told my father, is to touch our holy Polish earth. I know that no Jew loves our country more than you and our adorable Panna Tania, or has a truer national character. Still, to have a fine boy like yours educated by these city Jewesses is an error, a scandal. Give him one of our own. Salt of the earth. He will drink strength from her.

My father could not be indifferent to this line of reasoning or to his colleague's hierarchal position. Romantic nationalism was ascendant. My father's fine baritone voice could be heard singing marching songs commemorating the exploits of Piłsudski's brigade as often as Verdi arias. Such compliments as I received, when he took me for an evening stroll, were apt to be on my Polish, truly blond Sarmatian look. The Aryan look had not yet come into fashion in T. Nostalgia was directed to the Black Sea, whence came the Sarmatian warrior hordes, swords in hand, to settle our sainted Poland. Besides, the nurse's position was vacant again, and the surgeon had a candidate ready to start immediately.

Zosia was the oldest daughter of the assistant stationmaster in Drohobycz, a town some fifty kilometers from T. This functionary had been a corporal in the surgeon's battalion and later his patient. Having finished the first classes of *gimnazjum*, Zosia was helping out in a pastry shop. She needed to be placed.

Her golden beauty filled me with wonder; I think that something literally moved in my heart. To be sure, Tania was taller, her hair almost the same amber color. I loved the smell of Tania's perfume and powder, her furs that she was always happy to explain to me and let me play with and the softness of her hands that ended in long pale fingernails. But Zosia was soft and hard all at once and laughed with her head thrown back at everything that she or anyone else said. As soon as we were left alone—her interview must have been conducted days before she arrived, since it turned out that her little suitcase and bundles were already installed in her room—she swung me onto her shoulders, told me to hang on to her pigtails and set off at a run to inspect our garden. The raspberry bushes were heavy with fruit. She stuffed her mouth full and then mine and told me they were the sweetest she had eaten that summer. She thought the birds must be very respectful of my father to leave such fine berries alone and laughed her silver laugh when I informed her that they were covered with muslin except when the cook was ready to pick them.

From then on, it was understood that I would ride on her shoulders and hold her pigtails, which she would let down for me from the coil around her head as a reward for certain good actions. These included eating more than a third of what was served, especially if she helped just a little, chasing her at full gallop around the lawn, hanging by my knees from the jungle gym in the yard, not crying after my nap and being cleanly dressed and ready when my father offered to take me with him for an evening walk or to take Zosia and me on his round of house calls after office hours.

My father always used the same horse cab. He had confidence in the driver, who kept his carriage particularly clean and had a pair of horses capable of a sustained trot if we were going to a patient in a village outside T. I would sit with my father, holding his hand. Zosia would be on the jump seat, next to my father's black instrument bag, facing me, my knees squeezed between hers. When we arrived at a peasant's house, while my father was busy with the patient, she would ask for a glass of fresh buttermilk. If I drank it, my reward was a visit to the barn and a talk with the cattle and the hens. That was how I learned to caress the cheeks of a cow very slowly to make her my friend, to scatter grain for chickens correctly, and never to get within the reach of a chained dog.

For more important matters, there were other pacts and other rewards. The giant now came into my room to lean over me almost every night. I feared going to bed. Tania, if she was not going out, read to me; often she refused early invitations so that she could read a chapter she had promised to finish. Then, after Tania left, I would call Zosia. She left the door open that separated her room from mine, and she could hear me immediately. I listened for the sound of her bare feet with exultation. She would sing for me, and if I promised to be asleep after ten of her songs, she laughed, undid her pigtails and let me play with her loose hair. She sat on one of my little chairs, her head on the bed, hair spread over my quilt. I could run my fingers through it or pile it over my face. Her hair was very thick. It smelled slightly of soap. Zosia's own smell was a mixture of soap and fresh sweat; she teased me because I seldom sweated and would show me how wet her armpits became after our garden races. If I could not keep my promise, I told her. Zosia would sigh and kiss me, and sigh again or laugh. She would tell me I was her own cretin monster, her own nightmare, and let me bargain with her for more songs or caresses. If I chose caresses, I could touch her neck and ears. Then she would put her hands under my pajamas and stroke my chest, my stomach and my legs until I finally fell asleep, all the while sighing and laughing because I was so thin and because I was so ticklish and because I loved her too much.

My father had grown very concerned about the nightly apparitions. Was I hearing the Erlkönig's melodious blandishments? We decided that we should search for the giant and confront him. Together, we loaded the Browning pistol my father kept in his locked desk drawer. He showed me how to put a bullet in the chamber. So armed, we visited each room in the house. The wardrobes were opened; we poked behind coats and dresses and turned the linen in the drawers upside down. The smell of mothballs made us sneeze. There was no telling what shape the giant took in the day and where he might roost. To inspect the tenants' wing seemed too embarrassing; besides, it would not do to frighten them as well—our situation was already difficult. There remained only the cellar, with its barrels of pickles and sauerkraut, bins of potatoes and beets, and huge, empty leather trunks. These we examined one by one, I shining the flashlight, my father with his gun at the ready. Tania, who had declared at the start that we would find nothing, remained in the garden and read. Once again, she was right; in the day, the giant was invisible. My father felt my forehead and asked Zosia to keep me very quiet. It was the beginning of the fever that in a few days turned into whooping cough.

Since my birth, the Jewish holidays were the occasion of my maternal grandparents' annual visit to T. This autumn the holidays fell very early. My grandparents had not yet returned to Cracow for the winter from their property near S., a town to the north of T. Metternich once spent a night in S.; in his memoirs it is recorded that his enjoyment of the admirable natural beauty of the site and the surrounding countryside was spoiled by the large number of Jews living there. To relieve Tania of some of her responsibilities and to spend more time with me, they decided to come to us directly from the country, although my father had assured them I was not in danger. I was allowed to get up from bed to welcome them at the door. They arrived in their old, broad, open carriage. The coachman, who was my friend, was on the box. A wagon pulled by two horses followed with their luggage. As we had no stable, the horses would return to S., which made me cry with disappointment. My grandfather, rubbing his mustache against my face, patting me on the back, and crying a little himself, said that a man like me really needed his own carriage, that Jan would bring the horses back as soon as I was well enough to keep them busy going out every day; if I liked, I could even learn to drive the carriage myself.

Very tall, very straight, always dressed in black, with a mustache that was still black and white hair cut short in the "porcupine" style then favored by Polish gentry, my grandfather had a way of opening a world of infinite possibilities. His daughter Tania was his favorite; in her eyes, he was the paragon of men. On a word from him, she would bend consecrated rules governing my schedule and manners. As for my cautious, methodical and tender father, in his heart of hearts he thought of his father-in-law as a sort of benevolent centaur. In fact, the old gentleman was happier in the saddle than on the ground. Fondness for the myth (it was my father's habit to think of people closest to him as characters out of books, so that my grandmother, preoccupied with confitures and jams, was for him Countess Shcherbatskaya, and Bern, egging Tania on to some indiscretion, Rodolphe) and family piety eased the acceptance of my grandfather's very personal notions of hygiene in our modern and scientific household. My father was confiding his little Maciek to Chiron.

So it happened that, as soon as I was allowed to go out of the house again, grandfather introduced me to the delights of *miód*, a Polish liquor made of honey and thought by him to possess unique restorative properties. His carriage would wait before the gate. We would climb in, he reclining in the vast black leather seat, bareheaded (which was against the custom), a yellow cigarette in the corner of his mouth, and I on the box. Jan cracked his whip, and we would roll along to the first of my grandfather's favorite drinking cellars. He was of the view that *miód* could not be properly enjoyed elsewhere, certainly not in a café, that the steamy air of a good cellar, rich with odors of food, pickles and beer, in itself cleared one's lungs, and that his treatment was already working. He would order a carafe of *miód* and two glasses and pour a thimbleful for me. The idea was that we shared the work: I drank a sip and he took care of his glass and what was left in the carafe. There was another part of the deal: we ate two pairs of steamed sausages, work again being divided so that I ate one sausage while my grandfather polished off three. He showed me that both *miód* and steamed sausages went down faster if accompanied by horseradish—the red kind, mixed with beets, for me, and pure white, which made one's eyes water, for him. In the second and third cellars our system was the same, except that sometimes he would take herring and vodka for himself. In such a case, I could have a hard, honey-flavored cake to dip in my glass of *miód*.

As I was indeed becoming stronger and hardly coughed anymore, grandfather kept his promise about teaching me to drive. Tania was invited to come along: he called her his second-best pupil; I was to be the best. As soon as we left T. and reached one of the straight, long, white country roads, with fields of harvested rye and wheat stretching out on either side to distant lines of trees, Jan would rein in the horses, give a few turns to the brake crank, and Tania would climb on the box beside me. Then grandfather jumped on as well, told Jan to check the harness and get in the back, handed the reins to Tania, and released the brake. Tania touched the horses with the whip, and we would travel along at a clattering trot, my grandfather commenting on the smartness of the start and the length of the horses' gait. Finally, it was my turn. Grandfather seated me between his legs, Tania flushed and happy from the exercise was

still beside us, and the horses were settling
walk. The secret, grandfather would say,
the reins to me, was to keep the horses awake
the reins were in my hands, the pair usually stopp
after a few steps. Jan would join in the general hilarity,
then call out to the horses; they would start at a satisfactory pace while my grandfather showed me how to
keep the reins off the horses' backs, how one's hands
had to be steady and how one must never, never take
one's eyes off the road ahead. When we reached a cross-
road or a village, it was time for a lesson in turning the
horses or stopping. Sometimes, we bought freshly laid
eggs or white cow cheese from a peasant woman in a
village. She would cross herself at the sight of me driv-
ing the carriage and wish us God's blessings.

The holidays were over. The season of rains was beginning. Grandmother wanted to use the last few days
before their departure to set our house in proper order.
She bought new clothes for Zosia, whom she called her
big grandchild, inspected Tania's furs, had a long con-
ference with Tania about Bern and also about the cook
and the cook's dispendious ways with veal and finally
turned to putting up preserves. The jams and compotes
had been done directly after Yom Kippur; now was the
time for pickling cucumbers and preparing sauerkraut.

Grandmother's views on these subjects were firm. She
tolerated neither shortcuts nor excess in spices.
Tranquil-faced, with long skirts that almost touched the
floor, she was installed in an armchair at our kitchen
table. I was in her lap. The cabbage had already been
sliced and waited in white enamel vats to be salted,
sprinkled with peppercorns and bay leaves, and, last of
all, pressed. This was the moment I waited for. The
cook heaped the cabbage into wooden barrels, layer by

ɛr, and then Zosia and the chambermaid, because ꓹis was the task for the youngest and prettiest, hiked up their skirts above the knees, climbed in, and trod the mixture with bare feet to squeeze out the water. I often saw women's thighs in the dignified setting of our beach, but these bodies were different from Tania's and her friends'. Watching them, I felt a mixture of oppression and elation, as I did when Zosia let me caress her face and neck. My grandmother, whose powers of observation seldom flagged, said that I was a little rascal, that soon I would sell my grandmother and Tania for a good pair of legs, that I was the image of my grandfather, only more sly.

In fact, Tania resembled her father, and photographs of my mother showed the same almost angular features, the same tense and erect bearing. My grandmother had been known as a beauty, but she was all roundness, different from her daughters. Her once-black hair, now completely silver, washed only in rainwater to preserve its rich color, was worn in a large bun. She had large, languid brown eyes. Her nose was small and perfectly formed; a small red mouth that had never been touched by lipstick was set in a gentle, slightly suffering smile. She wore heavy necklaces, bracelets and rings, with which I was allowed to play under her supervision. In spite of her attractions, my grandfather had been irrepressibly and indiscreetly unfaithful, his activities extending beyond the normal Cracow nightlife world to peasants on his property and, during a terrifying interval that preceded my uncle's death, to my mother's and Tania's university friends. My grandmother did not pretend to be uninformed. She did not make scenes and she did not forgive. She was bitter, dignified and frequently sick. Her liver, kidneys and heart were fragile in ways that only my father fully understood. Toward

Tania, she was moody and demanding. She did not wish Tania to forget that her having remained unmarried was a bitter disappointment. Secretly, however, Tania's not finding a husband suited my grandmother: it meant she could devote her life to my father and me. Grandmother did not blame my father for my mother's death and considered him the worthiest of husbands and fathers. She would have liked him to marry Tania, according to tradition, but could she wish such a fate for that good man? Tania was her father's daughter, which in itself said plenty, and, to make matters worse, she was an intellectual, her mother thought. My grandmother was not very intelligent; intelligence, even if it was Tania's, made her nervous.

My grandfather used our last days together to train me in two new pursuits: jumping over fires and throwing a jackknife. Zosia played an important part in the fire game. Under grandfather's direction, she and I made piles of raspberry bush cuttings and dry flower stalks, carefully arranged in a straight line within a jump's distance. My grandfather lit the piles: on his signal, Zosia and I, holding hands, would jump or run over them and collapse breathless in each other's arms when we had finished. My grandfather waited till the flames were high. Then, having given me a hand salute, he would leap into flame after flame, emerging unscathed and triumphant.

We played with the jackknife sedately and alone. My grandfather wanted me to treat knives with the seriousness they deserved. He would draw a square in the dirt with the point and then small circles within the square. We stood a couple of paces away from the square, legs slightly apart and well balanced, and took turns throwing grandfather's heavy, much-used jackknife so as to make it land upright as close as possible to the center of each circle.

I would jump over fires with my grandfather during three more autumns; the game resumed with other companions, after the Warsaw uprising, in the frozen fields of the Mazowsze. By then, violent death was stalking him. But in that golden fall of 1937, while grandmother saw to the packing of their trunks and fussed over the train schedule, I was his hope, the little man to whom he was teaching all his secrets, the heir to his farms and forests and broken dreams.

I began to eat better. My father said such improvement often followed a long fever. New tastes appealed to me. Grandmother made little toasts in the kitchen fireplace, holding the bread over the fire with long tongs. On the toast she put a duck or chicken liver grilled by the same method. When she and grandfather returned to Cracow, Zosia took over. She would laugh and feel me for fat, like a hen at the market, as she prepared the fourth or fifth liver of the morning. My father thought it best to have my progress verified. We went to Lwów, the nearest university city, to consult a lung specialist. He wore a beard, a pince-nez and a green eyeshade. When I asked him whether he liked me, which was then my opening conversational move with strangers, he begged Tania to remind me that children were not to be heard except when replying to a grown-up's question. The professor's stethoscope was very cold, the auscultation interminable; then Tania and I were asked to step into the waiting room while my father received his colleague's opinion. He emerged from the consultation room radiant. According to the great man, my lungs were clear but I behaved like a spoiled girl. I should be in the fresh air as much as

possible. It would make my head as clear as my lungs.
In consequence, my father required that the daily schedule be changed. So long as the weather continued sunny
and dry, I would go sledding with Zosia every morning.
Reading, piano lessons and such like could wait until
the afternoon. A season of enchantment began. On the
other side of T., beyond the railroad station, was a hill
sloping to the riverbank. A horse-drawn sleigh took Zosia and me and our sled there every morning and came
back at noon to fetch us. We slid from the highest point,
down the steepest slope, at first Zosia steering and I
lying on top of her. Then she taught me to steer by
leaning or dragging my boot on the snow, and she
helped only if we were headed into a clump of trees.
We were alone; older children had classes, and the hill-
side was too distant for nurses who had to pull their
charges behind them. Zosia said this was our kingdom;
I was the king and she the queen. We made snowmen
and brought gilded paper crowns to put on their heads.

Tania and my father were gratified by the results: I
looked sturdier and I was growing. I stopped talking
about the giant and after one story from Tania was prepared to say good-night and close my eyes. Exercise
and good food alone were not responsible for this particular improvement. Since my fever fell, and my father
no longer thought it necessary to look in on me in the
night to listen to my breathing, Zosia had told me that
I could sleep in her bed. She was sure that no giant
would think of looking for me there. Therefore, as soon
as Tania had given me the last of her sleep-well kisses,
I would tiptoe into Zosia's room. She would be laughing or growling giant noises until I slipped under her
huge goose feather bed. Our old agreements still held:
I could play with her hair and touch her on the face and
on the neck. I could also put my arms around her, and

she would caress me until I fell asleep. Then if I thought
the giant might come, I would quickly awaken her. She
would be all warm and wet from sleep, often her night-
shirt had worked its way up, and when she pressed me
against her I felt her naked legs, her stomach. She would
talk to me very softly: giants and mean dwarfs were
cowards. They might pick on a little boy all alone. But
I was a big boy now, and, with her, I would never be
alone. I would tell her I was still afraid and tug at her
shirt so that as much of me as possible was right next
to her, inside her smell and warmth. She would laugh.
I was a little rascal and had to learn to behave, but in
the meantime she would tickle me until I was quite sure
the giant was not coming that night, and this worked
so well that she agreed that, from then on, as soon as
I came into her bed, she would pull up her shirt or let
me creep under it, and I could touch her as much as I
wished if I promised never, never to tickle her, even
though she could tickle me as much as she liked. We
honored this pact. Often, after she had fallen asleep, I
stayed very quiet, with my eyes closed, and passed my
hands over her breasts and her stomach. Her naked but-
tocks were pressed against my legs. My heart beat very
fast; then I too would fall asleep. And, though the fear
is still vivid in my memory when I think of the door to
my father's study and the porcelain stove beside it, the
giant has never returned in my dreams again.

The next March the Anschluss took place. My father
listened to the BBC news explaining names and places.
The fabric of his youth was unraveling. Hitler on Kärnt-
nerstrasse! Paradoxically, my father canceled the cruise
that was to have taken Tania, him and me to the Med-
iterranean that summer. He said it was no time to be
so far from home. Tania and he argued. She told him

it was precisely the time to leave Poland, while it was still possible; there was talk that one could get visas for Australia and Brazil. My father said that was all right for the grandparents and her; they could even have me with them for a while, and I could return to T. when everybody felt calm again. But his place, his duty, were in Poland. Tania said he was a fool. How could he imagine my grandfather in Australia at the head of the family? If we were going abroad we needed him.

My father's uniforms were taken out of the storage wardrobe. He inspected them and had two pairs of britches taken in—the diet he had been following for kidney stones made him lose weight. He and Tania argued about where the August vacation would be spent. My father thought I should be at my grandparents' place in the country. Tania said she wasn't going; he could take me there himself. But that was impossible: he was substituting for the Catholic surgeon, who had already been called up on maneuvers. They settled on M., a popular spa some two hours away, famous for its mud and warm mineral water. The water would be good for my father's stones; he could join us on weekends. Bern was also going and would look after us when we were alone.

In M., we lodged in a brown wooden hotel standing in its own small park. A short distance from the park, down a shady boulevard, was the *Kurhaus*. In front of it was a kiosk for the orchestra. Off to the right one drank the water through angled glass straws. Zosia and I shared a room. Next door was Tania's room, with a large balcony, armchairs and an awning. When my father came, he took whatever room near us was free. Zosia wore blue cotton skirts with white blouses that Tania had imposed instead of a nurse's uniform. I had sailor suits; I seemed to be always propelling a hoop

before me. Tania had never been more elegant. She
wore long beige pleated skirts with sailor tops edged in
navy blue (she claimed these were to go with my suits),
dresses of white and blue and gray raw silk, and little
hats, like helmets, of matching straw. Bern was often
with us. He had an automobile the top of which could
be taken down: a Skoda. He drove it himself. Tania
claimed that he went too fast, and swore Zosia and me
to secrecy. My father must not know about the risks we
were taking on our drives through the woods near M.
On Saturdays, my father appeared, arriving by train,
sad, tired, ready for a good time. He held my hand on
our walks and asked that I sit next to him when we
went to a café for sweets or ices. At the very end of
August, he came in the middle of the week: Tania and
Bern were going to Lwów to see a cabaret act that was
essential and could not be missed. It was the first time
Tania had left me alone with my father. He asked me
to come to his room as soon as I woke up. There were
things he had to tell me. It turned out that he was privy
to the secrets of an English spy named Alan, who had
learned from a Chinaman by the name of Tung Ting
the true story of the kidnapping of the last empress of
China. The story was involved and seemingly endless;
he told it to me from then on in installments, on Sunday
mornings.

Brusquely, August ended. We returned to T. Talk
about Germany displaced most other conversation. For
the first time, I heard the word "Wehrmacht." There
were jokes about the Polish army: How many times can
the same tank pass before Rydz-Śmigły reviewing in the
course of one parade? Answer: Exactly the number of
times our only airplane can fly over his head during that
parade. A few weeks later, Germany occupied the Su-
detenland; we bravely sliced off a piece of Czechoslovakia

without losing a single Polish life; soldiers returned with wreaths of wildflowers around their necks. Beneš resigned and was replaced by Hácha. Now, there were jokes about Hácha's name—the last prewar jokes I remember. Kristallnacht happened and was spoken about in embarrassed whispers. Rydz-Śmigły and Beck, Poland's new leaders, would know where to draw the line; nationalism was not the same as lower-class bestiality. There were certain subjects that my father and Tania did not want to discuss before Zosia. We would both be sent out of the room on some indispensable errand. Less than one year later came September 1939, and it was all over.

II

I T HAD BEEN RAINING VERY HARD FOR MORE THAN TWO
weeks. We heard that the river had overflowed and the
bridge might be washed away. Our cellar flooded. My
grandfather tipped the barrels of pickles and sauerkraut
and put boards under them so they would not stand in
water. He emptied potatoes and beets from the bins,
and we stored them in bags that he and Tania carried
into the kitchen and laundry room. Sacks of flour and
rice also had to be moved, along with bags of dried
beans that were less heavy. They said I could help with
them.

Later that day, I was at the window of my father's
study and watched water, now almost as high as the
sidewalk, streaming in the direction of the railroad station. Across the street, in the house that belonged to
the older of my father's Jewish colleagues, were stationed the SS. German troops overran eastern Poland
in June 1941, after Hitler broke the Molotov-Ribbentrop
pact and attacked Russia. Dr. Kipper had not left with
the medical staff when the Russians evacuated the hospital during the days of panic preceding the Germans'
entry into T. Families were not allowed on the evacu-
ation train to Russia, and my father and the younger
Jewish doctor had left alone, very quietly. While he was
getting his things together, I lay face down on the white
rubber-covered couch in his examination room, crying,

out of breath, unable to speak. Dr. Kipper refused to
leave without Mrs. Kipper. The chief Russian doctor
called him a deserter and said he would have him executed, but there wasn't time. Instead, Dr. and Mrs.
Kipper were shot by the Germans a few days later, together with some other Jews. It was all done in the early
afternoon, in the field on the other side of T. where
Zosia and I used to go sledding, but they brought the
bodies back to town in a truck and rounded up some
other Jews to unload it. Earlier in the day, a good part
of T.'s Catholic population had come out into the streets
to greet the German soldiers. It was all very gay; these
well-dressed warriors on their trucks and motorcycles,
with leather cases and field glasses hanging from their
necks, were a nice change after the shabby, bedraggled
Russians retreating from the front. There were girls
handing flowers to them. They were happy to have the
Russians gone. Zosia wanted to take me on her shoulders to watch, but Tania absolutely forbade it, and she
said Zosia wasn't even to go there herself. The roundup
of the Jews, the shooting and then the corpses dumped
on the street made people more cautious. One couldn't
yet be sure that this was just something between Germans and Jews.

The rain became heavier. In a short time, the sidewalks disappeared under the water. The SS rushed out
from the Kipper house in shorts, without their black
boots, holding their carbines over their heads. They
milled about for a while in knee-high water. Then the
Feldwebel shouted an order, and they all ran off in a
single file toward the station.

I went back to the kitchen. Tania was cooking lunch.
My grandfather smoked. He had recently acquired a
new sort of cigarette, which was made like a two-part
tube. One inserted tobacco into the thin paper part with

a little metal pusher that resembled a lady's curling iron.
It was important to be careful, or the paper would tear.
He was teaching me how to do it correctly. The other
tube was like a cigarette holder. My grandmother was
wrapped in her fur coat against the humidity. She
wanted to know what we would do when the kitchen
flooded. Tania assured her that God would look after
us in this as in every other adversity; besides, what
difference did it make? We wouldn't be staying in the
house much longer.

My grandparents came to T. in September 1939 to
escape from the Germans and to be near us in this time
of danger. They lived in our house. Relations between
the mother and the daughter had not improved, and
now practically all the work of the house fell to Tania.
Most often, she refused grandmother's offers of aid,
saying that she needed real help, someone to do something, and not instructions about how this or that should
be done. Grandfather alternated between asking Tania
to think what kind of example she was setting for me
and laughing and teasing. He claimed that this was real
peasant-woman talk and that Tania should be congrat-
ulated on her progress in learning proletarian manners.

Before the Russians took him with them, my father
had been careful to stay out of this sort of family dis-
cussion. He would only say that he felt guilty about how
tired Tania was. It was he, after all, who had decided,
very soon after the Russians arrived in 1939, that we
could keep Zosia if she was willing to help a little
with the housework and that all the others had to be let
go. One could not carry on like bourgeois, he explained, especially with the grandparents right there.
Landowners were considered the worst class. One denunciation would send us all to Siberia. He joked that

we would not find the House of the Dead a satisfactory family residence.

Now Zosia was gone as well. Aryans were no longer allowed to work for Jews. Zosia cried, saying this had nothing to do with us, that I was her child. She wanted to stay. She would become Jewish like me. But her father came from Drohobycz and asked to speak to Tania. He told her it was high time his child stopped wiping the rear end of a little Jew bastard. He was prepared to let bygones be bygones, but there had to be compensation. What kind of a future could Zosia have with the smell of Jew all about her? Fortunately, my grandfather was out of the house. Tania asked Zosia's father to wait at the railroad station and please to remember next time he called on us to come to the kitchen door. She went to get her beaver coat and hat and gave them to Zosia and also gave her money. Grandmother too wanted to give Zosia a fur, but Zosia cried very hard and refused, and instead grandmother gave her the ring with little diamonds she always wore on her second finger. Then Zosia packed her things. She asked to wait for my grandfather, but Tania said to run along, that all this crying and saying good-bye was going to make me regress permanently to being a two-year-old.

Tania turned out to be right about the house. A few days after the flood receded, a German officer presented himself, very politely asked Tania if she was the owner and told her that we must move out by the end of the next day. The house was needed for Gestapo headquarters. We could take our clothes and personal items; everything else was to remain. An inventory would be made. He suggested she be present to make sure that everything was quite in order and said it was pleasant in this part of the world to hear German spoken correctly.

Our tenants were also ordered to leave. Pan Kramer came to see Tania and told her that he was embarrassed to propose such a thing, but if we wished, we could move together. He knew of an apartment near the market, a couple of houses from his shop. It was very modest, not the sort of thing she had ever seen, but it was available and it was furnished. The old lady who lived there was willing to give it up and go to live with her children. The rent was too high for the Kramers alone. Since we were old neighbors, perhaps we would not mind sharing. They were very quiet, spent most of the day in the shop, and Irena and I could play together. My grandfather was consulted and he agreed. There were no apartments for Jews in T.; Jews were all being thrown out. He would see the man who had stabled his horses about carting our things.

The new apartment was in a house that was four stories high. We were to live on the third floor, which was hard on grandmother because of her heart. One passed through a gateway wide enough for a horse-drawn cart into a rectangular courtyard. Above it, balconies on which the apartments opened ran around each floor, linked by stairs. Our apartment consisted of three rooms and a large kitchen that my grandmother declared was quite good. The three Kramers were to sleep in one room; Tania insisted they take the largest one. My grandparents had the room next to them, where there were two beds. Tania and I took the living room; she would sleep on the couch and I on a folding cot we could open at night. We discovered there was no running water; one got it from the pump in the courtyard. Pan Kramer showed me how to work the pump, with short strokes at first to get the water to flow and then slow and steady; that was how to do it without getting tired. Irena and I were to be responsible for the water: that was how one became careful not to waste it.

We made yet another discovery. There were no toilets, just one room on each floor with a sort of box and an enamel bucket inside it for all the tenants to share. One could use it or one could use a chamber pot. One emptied the bucket or chamber pot in the outhouse in the yard. One could also go to the outhouse in the first place. I asked Tania which she intended to do. In reply, she slapped my face very hard, right in front of Pan and Pani Kramer and Irena. It was the first time that she had ever hit me; she had fired Zosia's immediate predecessor and made her leave in the middle of the night because that Panna had slapped me.

This time it was grandmother who flew to my defense. She said she was ashamed; Tania should move in with Bern if that was how she meant to behave. Grandfather told them both to stop and asked me to come for a walk with him.

I was crying, and I noticed that he was crying a little also. All the same, he told me crying was no use. Everything had changed. We were in for a difficult time. People would act very differently because they were afraid and confused; even he was afraid. He thought what I must learn was to watch very carefully and try to understand things as much as possible with this in mind. He would try to help, but I had to remember that grandmother was sick, that they were both old and that Tania was the one who would take care of me until the war ended and my father came back. Afterward we walked to the end of the street, where there was an empty lot with piles of gravel and larger stones and a lumberyard that seemed deserted. Still farther off was the river. Some Catholic boys, older than I, were throwing stones, aiming at trees. We stopped to watch. They threw very hard and accurately. I asked grandfather if he would teach me to throw like that. He said that he couldn't; being a bad thrower himself was something he had regretted all his life. There was another skill, though, that was equally useful. We went to the marketplace and bought some thick red rubber and a patch of leather. Then we returned to a pile of gravel in the empty lot. My grandfather cut a low, forked branch from a tree, peeled it, threaded the rubber strip through two holes he made in the leather, and then fastened the rubber to the fork. He explained that he had just made a slingshot and that we were going to practice using it right then, and as often as we got a chance, but I must not tell grandmother about it, and I must not aim at houses because I could break a window. When I got good at it, we would try shooting crows.

Later that afternoon, Bern came to see us. He brought a bouquet of yellow asters for my grandmother. She thanked him and asked if they were to match her new Jewish star. He also brought cigarettes and vodka and said he didn't know which was for Tania and which was for my grandfather. Everybody laughed at that, and my grandfather told him he was sure the cigarettes had to be for Tania; if Bern had intended to bring Tania liquor he would have brought champagne.

When the bottle was almost empty, and the Kramers had gone to their room, Bern said that he had been asked to become a director at the Jewish community office the Germans were forming and that he would do it. It might be a way to keep his *garçonnière* and help us with all sorts of things like ration cards; he might be able to get Tania a job. It would become dangerous to be unemployed. He did not care what people thought; if he did not do it, the Jewish-question people at the *Kommandantur* would pick some illiterate black-market profiteer instead. The only other solution for him was the forest, but it was hard to make contact with the partisans, and besides, he did not want to leave Tania and the rest of us without any protection.

It was true that, quite apart from what perhaps went on between him and Tania, Bern was now our only friend. The Catholic surgeon, like my father, had made his way back to T. when the Polish front collapsed in 1939 but had not been evacuated to Russia. He had been polite to Tania each time she went to see him at the hospital, but Tania said she had a feeling her welcome was wearing out. He had told her right away that it was impossible to give her work at the hospital. If my father had only listened to him before the war and we had all converted, the situation might be different. Now it was much too late even for that; he was sorry that we had brought such troubles on ourselves. Of course, we weren't really responsible; it was the other Jews, who did not know how to lead a Polish national life. Unfortunately, it was too late for that sort of distinction as well. As far as medication for her respected mother was concerned, professional courtesy was his battle cry, Germans or no Germans. She could have anything she wanted. Tania noted, and mentioned it each time she told the story, that the last time she went for grandmother's prescription he said good-bye without kissing her hand.

Bern told us that he had learned on the telephone from a colleague in Lwów that the *Kommandantur* there had given the Jewish community office orders to move all the Jews into a ghetto, like the ones in Warsaw and Cracow. It was no laughing matter. People would have to live squeezed together like sardines. It would make us think the new lodgings we shared with these very decent Kramers were luxuriously spacious. He hoped it

would not come to that in T. We already had the arm-
bands, the yellow star and the curfew. If the Jewish
community office acted responsibly, and our dear café
intellectuals for once avoided provoking the Poles, perhaps we could remain as we were. This way of talking
was new, and Tania and my grandfather teased Bern
about it, saying he was using very modern Polish. We
had always referred to Poles who were Catholics simply
as Catholics, because after all we too thought we were
Poles. But the mention of the curfew made them remember the hour; it was time for Bern to leave. Tania
went out with him, saying she would accompany him
as far as the corner.

When Tania returned, grandmother said she was glad
she was sick and would not live long anyway. She had
been one of four sisters; people said they were all good-
looking; now only she was left. When she was a young
girl, she could have everything she wanted. Then when
her father lost his money, my grandfather performed the
only good action of his life: he paid his father-in-law's
debts. The two real children she had were dead; Tania
had never been her child. Now my grandfather could
be proud of how she had turned out. Just like his
women. This was enough misfortune in one life, and
yet she didn't mind the hovel we were in, or wearing a
star or an armband, or being beaten or shot like those
poor Kippers. When she was ten, she had seen a pogrom. Ukrainian peasants pulled beautiful Jewish men
by their beards, violated young girls, beat everybody.
Thank God, they had not come into their house, but
she had seen and heard. She didn't think Germans could
do worse. But never, in all that time, or anytime until
now, had she heard anyone talk as shamelessly as Bern.
My grandfather remained silent. Tania looked very tired
and very calm. After a while, she turned to my grand-

mother and said, You don't know yet what is shameless, you don't know yet what we will do, just wait, you will see before you die.

A short time later, Bern got a job for Tania in the Wehrmacht supply depot. They needed someone who could speak and write German perfectly and also do some typing, and finally told the Jewish community office to supply such a person. There did not seem to be any qualified Aryans in T. This development made our situation very much better—we had become the dependents of an essential worker—but it left me very much alone. Grandmother was sicker than usual, and grandfather had to take care of her. Because everything was rationed, he spent a good part of the day buying provisions in the regular stores, where one had to wait in lines, and also pursuing his private connections through which he could get good milk and eggs and sometimes calves' liver. Grandmother had a liver ailment; it was recommended that she eat only lean food, and calves' liver was both lean and very strengthening.

I began to spend all the time when grandfather and grandmother did not need me with Irena or the older boys in the building. There was no school for Jews anymore. The boys and I played hide-and-seek in the lumberyard at the end of the street. No workmen ever seemed to be there. We built a shack where we could sit when it rained or when we wanted to talk. We talked about women; they explained how one could shove it in between a girl's legs so she would bleed or into her rear end. In either case, it had to hurt. Women bled every month anyway. They used paper to stop it, but sometimes they couldn't. The blood was called *kurwa*. The worst insult was to call somebody *kurwamać* or *kurwysyn*. That was mother or son of that blood. You could shove it into a woman when she was bleeding and women liked it, but it was a very dirty thing to do. The boys wanted to know if I had already shoved it into Irena. One of them had seen her in the latrine. They thought I should try, when she was asleep. All I had to worry about was the blood that her mother would see in the morning. There was a song that could be adapted to the name of each of us and to the name of each girl we knew. They would sing it about Irena and me: Maciek, Maciek, an officer made Irena an offer, I will shove in my two-meter, you will bleed a whole liter. She cries it's hard, it's hard, but this just makes him fart. She cries now I bleed, but he pays no heed. We marched up and down an alley in the lumberyard, taking turns being in the lead and being named in the song with a girl whom one of us was thought to like or who was in his family.

The empty lot and the lumberyard were also, after they got out of their school, the territory of many Catholic boys. They played tag ball and practiced throwing stones at trees, just as they had the day grandfather and I had watched them. When they wanted a space we were in, they would yell that all Jews and other garbage must disappear. We began to throw stones at one another. I would use my slingshot once or twice and then run away. The older boys stayed and fought. I was discovering that I liked to hurt others but was afraid of being hurt myself.

One day, the Catholic boys came in much greater numbers and said they would kill us. It would be a permanent Jew curfew. They had big rocks, the size of fists, and sticks with nails in them. From then on, we went to the lumberyard only during their school hours. We would urinate on the piles of stones they used. It served them right to get Jewish piss on their hands.

I was reading the books of Karl May. Bern had

brought them to me, saying they were just the thing to fill my time when grandfather was so busy. Old Shatterhand had no fear of Indians; he liked and understood them very well, and yet he killed them pitilessly. Laughing, Bern pointed out to me that Old Shatterhand often killed fifteen redskins in a row, although his Colt .45 only held six bullets. I was not discouraged by Bern's scoffing. Probably, May did not bother mentioning each time Old Shatterhand reloaded. Irena liked these books too. When we played, she would be the only squaw left alive in a village where I had just exterminated all the braves. She would plead to be spared; she deserved to be punished for the crimes of her tribe, but she was very young and did not want to die. I would tie her up, sometimes to the chair, and sometimes spread-eagle on Tania's couch. Then we would argue about whether she should be tortured, for instance by having the soles of her feet burned, or whipped with my lasso, or released at once to become my servant. It was lucky that Irena looked like a squaw. She had black hair and black eyes and a broad nose. She wasn't very big; I was almost as tall as she and I could wrestle her down when we fought.

Irena found a book called *In the Opium Den* that her father kept in the back of his shop. We read it in Tania's and my room, where nobody could see us. A German living in China uses opium. He smokes it lying on a low couch, dressed only in a silk kimono. The German's skin has become all yellow from the opium; he is very thin. His Chinese mistress kneels on the floor next to the couch, also dressed only in a kimono, which falls off her shoulders. Her breasts are small but have large nipples. The German holds her breast and pinches her nipple very hard and explains that he no longer wants to do it; he just wants to puff on his pipe and

dream about how they have done it in the past. He tells
her his dreams. Then, one evening he feels the stirring
of a desire. Near the couch on a little table lies a box
studded with precious stones. He asks her to open it
and take the ivory-handled razor inside it. Then he
makes her cut one nipple with the razor. He wants the
blood to run first on his chest and then into his mouth.
Irena said we should play opium den. She could get her
mother's bathrobe to use as a kimono, and we would
pretend about the razor. Her breasts were already round,
like two bumps.

My grandmother felt much worse, and then after
leeches and cups were applied directly over her liver to
relieve the congestion, she improved. Her room no longer had to be darkened. I was allowed to sit with her.
She told stories about the country, when I used to visit
them in the summer. She wanted to know if I remembered the rabbits and the goose she kept especially for
me, and about picking mushrooms. It was all very vivid
in her mind, in what direction we had gone for a drive
on a particular afternoon when my father came to see
us, in what clothes she had dressed me, and the day I
learned to like cold raspberry soup. She told me about
my uncle, and how he died. She said my mother had
looked just like him; they were both too gentle and too
good. She was glad I took after my grandfather. We
were living through a time that was not made for good
people.

I liked being with her. Irena now had to be at the
shop almost all the time; her parents did not want to be
separated from her in case there was another roundup.
For the same reason, grandfather no longer allowed me
to go out to play with the boys. The first *Judenaktion*
had just taken place in T. It was done one morning by
the SS, with some Polish policemen in civilian clothes

and a lot of Jewish militiamen. I was in the lumberyard with the boys when it happened. Some of them ran home when the shouting began, but I and a couple of others were too scared; we hid between a large stack of boards and the fence. We could watch from there. The Germans went into one house after another, yelling in German, *Alle Juden heraus!* All Jews out! It took a long while, and then people began to pour into the street, where the Jewish militiamen lined them up in an orderly way. I saw my grandparents and Pan and Pani Kramer and Irena, all standing together. Then the Po-lish policemen began to check everybody's papers and divide people into two groups. They put my grandpar-ents, the Kramers and some other people off to the side and pushed the other group toward trucks that had meanwhile arrived at the end of the street. A woman I did not know suddenly broke away from a file that was climbing on a truck and rushed to the other end of the street, where some large cement pipes were stacked. She crawled into one of them and would not come out, al-though the Germans were ordering her to. For a while, everything was still. Then two militiamen came and poked at her with long sticks until she appeared, on hands and knees, at the other end. There, the Germans kicked and beat her and finally got her on the truck, which was al-ready quite full, and drove away. The militiamen and the Polish police remained and told the Jews who were still in the street to clean up.

When I returned, my grandfather said I was right to remain hidden because it all had happened when I wasn't with them, but the important thing, in fact, was for me not to be alone. This particular roundup was against Jews without working papers or proof that they were dependents of workers. If they had caught me alone, they probably would have taken me too because

I had no papers and nobody would have spoken up for me; then grandmother and grandfather would have had to follow, to be with me. I said it made no sense that they had to go with me if it was right for me to hide in the lumberyard instead of running to them, but grandfather explained that they had already lived their lives; they would be quite willing to go if I could stay with Tania. The thing we had to try hard to prevent was for me to be taken alone or to be left alone if they and Tania were taken.

Tania appeared almost immediately after the roundup was over, very frightened. She had heard about it while it was still going on; the Germans in her office told her to go home right away to make sure we were safe and gave her a document that was an order saying we were not to be disturbed, which she was to leave with us. We would talk later; in the meantime, she had to go back to work. This was typical of Tania now—she was always saying we would talk when she came back from the office. As soon as she had gotten her job, Tania brought home a typewriter and practiced every evening after work. She said if she learned to type quickly and accurately she would become indispensable. She sat at the table in our room copying page after page of a German novel. Then, to practice dictation, she had my grandfather read aloud from the novel fairly fast, and she tried to keep up with him on the typewriter. One day, she said it was enough; she was the best the Germans had. They gave her a special pass, so that she didn't have to respect the curfew, and often she worked very late. Sometimes, she was on duty all night and only came home in the morning to change her clothes.

That evening, however, she returned early. She brought canned pâté, a bottle of vodka, and chocolate for grandmother and me, although grandmother was supposed to avoid sweets. She also brought a canned ham for the Kramers and chocolate for Irena. After dinner, when we were in my grandparents' room, she said she wanted to tell us an important secret. She had a German friend. He was in love with her. He wasn't a Nazi, he wasn't even a soldier anymore, although he wore a uniform, because he had lost an arm in a factory accident. He was very good at organizing army supplies, so he was important and influential. If we were lucky, if grandfather behaved reasonably, her friend would save us. He was already risking his life for Jews. Bern had found a way to get to the partisans; this German friend, Reinhard, was equipping him for the forest. He was even going to give Bern a rifle and ammunition and drive him to the rendezvous in his own car. We would meet Reinhard when the time came. She wanted grandfather and grandmother to think of me and for once to concentrate on what was really happening around them. She didn't care what others would think. Jews in T. and everywhere else in Poland were as good as dead, but she intended to live and to save us, and this was the only way.

They knew they could not shout because of the Kramers, so the news all came out very slowly and very quietly. There came a silence, and then my grandfather said that Tania was wrong, it was not the only way. If the Germans won the war, then her way led nowhere—in the end, we would be killed just like everybody else, only perhaps a little later. And if the Germans lost, then surviving her way was no good. There was enough money, if we sold grandmother's jewelry piece by piece, to get a peasant family to hide us and feed us as long as the war lasted. He would begin looking for the right people immediately.

Tania had been crying, but at once she stopped. She spoke again very softly and very slowly. She said that no peasant family would take all four of us; we would have to be separated; and if peasants took us, it would be to get hold of our money and our jewels. Afterward, they would sell us to the Germans. There had already been such cases near Lwów. Jews found families to hide them so they would not have to go to the ghetto, and after a week with their saviors they were denounced and shot. Waiting in some boarded-up cellar until the Gestapo came to get us was not for her. We could trust Reinhard; anyway, there was no use arguing. Reinhard had told her that he would take care of all of us and that he would not, under any conditions, allow her to leave.

So Tania won the argument, and so far as we four were concerned, it was all now in the open. Bern came to say good-bye. It was awkward, until Tania said that she would be there when Reinhard and he drove off the next morning. Then Bern understood that what she was doing was no longer a secret, and he said that Tania was the best of daughters and friends, that she was brave, and that Reinhard was probably the only decent man in T., present company excepted but all Jews included. Thinking about him, and the possibility that perhaps he was killing someone like him, would be the only thing that could spoil the joy of killing Germans once he got to the forest. Tania told us later that she helped to wrap Bern like a bundle in blankets and cover him with other bundles in the back of Reinhard's car. My grandparents and I never saw him again. Grandmother sometimes mentioned him, saying she hoped he was doing well in the forest; she was glad she was no longer obliged to speak to him. Grandfather would laugh; according to him poor Bern had no need to be worried about shooting good Germans; Bern would never manage to shoot anybody, good or bad.

All the time we were waiting for good news, and none came. We listened to the Wehrmacht radio. It told us that Europe was theirs, all the way to the Spanish border. They were before Moscow; the British army in Africa was wax in Rommel's hands. They would invade England. Sometimes we could catch the BBC. Its story was not very different. My grandfather stopped making jokes about Napoleon and field marshal snow. Jews were rounded up almost every week now, for different purposes. Always, there would be the SS in their rich uniforms and shiny leather, Polish policemen who understood Jews and could not be fooled by their tricks, and Jewish militiamen with long sticks hurrying people along, throwing their possessions into the street. They were now taking away men under thirty, men and women over sixty-five, and sometimes unemployed Jews, even if the head of the family had working papers. In our building, members of families had been separated. The Kramers thought they would hide Irena behind the boxes of supplies in their storeroom if there was time; the disadvantage was that people found hiding were always beaten and sometimes shot directly after the beating.

The noise of the roundups remained in one's ears a long time after it was all over: first would be the announcement *Achtung Judenaktion*, then the Germans yelling monotonously *Alle Juden heraus*, the Poles yelling in Polish, and Jewish militiamen yelling in Polish and Yiddish, people wailing. From time to time, there was also the barking of police dogs. We speculated about what was done with the people who were taken away. If they were put on trucks and driven out of T., they were likely to be shot in a wood a little distance away. That is what peasants who lived in that direction said. Those who were herded to the railroad station and put on trains might be going anywhere. There was talk of a camp in Bełzec, near Lublin, of factory work in Germany, of Wehrmacht brothels, of consolidation in ghettos of the large cities like Lwów, Łódź and Warsaw. Tania said that none of them would ever return; it did not matter where they died. Our papers guaranteed that we would not be touched. She was right. When she or, if she was at work, grandfather showed them to the police, they would tell us to return quietly to our apartment. We began to be treated with suspicion by our neighbors, even the Kramers, although Tania never brought home food anymore without bringing a package for them as well.

New rules required Jews to step off the sidewalk if a German was approaching. Whoever didn't move fast enough was beaten; sometimes people were executed right on the spot. Polish youths thought they were entitled to the same respect. It became common to see them chasing Jews of any age, hitting them with canes or throwing stones at them. Polish police did not interfere; occasionally, order was restored by a German Feldgendarmerie patrol. My grandfather told me to remember these scenes: I was seeing what happens if one is turned into a small animal like a rabbit. He now regretted having been a hunter all his life. When Tania heard him, she shrugged her shoulders. According to her, Catholic youths beating Jews with canes was nothing new; National Democratic students had amused themselves just that way in the corridors of the university in Cracow in her time.

Since the beginning of the winter, there had been rumors that a ghetto would be established in T. They became more insistent. My grandfather thought it was unlikely; there were too few Jews left to justify the bother. A couple of good roundups would be enough to kill them all. Tania reported that Reinhard was less sure of what might happen. He explained that the general rule called for all Jews to be in ghettos, and that the Jewish-question people would not be deterred by practical considerations. On the other hand, in the case of other small towns, Jews had been sent to big-city ghettos. That meant we might be sent to Lwów. Either possibility, ghetto in T. or ghetto in Lwów, worried him a lot. He thought that, once we were inside, it would be very difficult for him to create better conditions for us; he was not even sure that he could protect us. We supposed, although Tania did not say so, that he was also afraid he would be less free to see her.

At last, he decided that, until the situation became clearer, he would personally hide us in T. Incredibly, what made him think that it would be easy to hide us was that his daughter was coming to spend the Christmas holidays with him. She loved him; her mother had died when she was little; she would accept the situation. He had complete trust in her and so should we, Tania told us; his life and his daughter's were at stake just as much as ours. He would take a larger apartment for his daughter, and Tania and I would move there too. My grandparents would live in his. We would be in the same building, but we would have to remember that we were hidden. There would be no going out and no seeing one another until he was able to make a better arrangement.

My grandfather said that Reinhard was right about avoiding the ghetto at all cost, but he was not going to hide behind a sofa in a German officer's apartment while other arrangements were thought of, because nothing would come of this thinking. And Tania was right about peasants selling Jews. Grandfather would instead get Aryan papers for us. He knew how genuine or forged birth and baptismal certificates and all the German-invented nonsense documents could be bought. Then at least grandmother, he and I could leave for Warsaw and sink into some obscure hole. Provided we avoided Catholics who knew us, they would be just another up-rooted old couple, waiting out the war with their orphaned grandchild. Tania could follow as soon as Reinhard came to his senses.

He did get the papers, but the scheme could not work. Grandmother was too sick for the discomforts and risks of travel, and certainly too sick to take care of me in Warsaw. How grandfather could take care of both of us was the question Tania asked over and over. She gave us a message from Reinhard: let the grandfather go first and find his bearings in Warsaw; we will send the grandmother and the boy when both he and they are ready. This time all three of them agreed that Reinhard was right. We would be separated, but only for a short while, and there was nothing else that could be done.

My grandfather could not leave from T. by train; he was too well known to go to the station, buy a ticket and board the train. These actions were all forbidden to Jews. Once recognized, he would be arrested and probably shot. Reinhard would not hear about peasants' carts or professional passers who might take him to the Lwów or Drohobycz station. One night, well after the curfew, Reinhard came to pick him up. My grandfather was ready, and we all stood together at the entranceway to the yard. We said good-bye; we were all crying. Then Reinhard got out of his car, kissed my grandmother's hand and took grandfather's suitcase. He was almost as tall as grandfather and wrapped in a military coat. They were going to Lwów. From there, grandfather could take a train with relative safety.

It was common knowledge that the greatest dangers for Jews living on Aryan papers were being unmasked by the Polish police or denounced to the Polish or German police—either by Polish neighbors, indignant at the usurpation by some Rosenduft or Rozensztajn of an honorable name and identity, or by dissatisfied extortionists. Germans could not distinguish an assimilated Jew from a Pole unless the Jew had a face that looked like a Nazi caricature. They caught Jews trying to pass for Poles only if assisted by the Polish police or by a denunciation or if they recognized the Aryan papers presented by the Jew as a forgery. Perhaps because Germans were so deficient in this domain, a profitable profession had sprung up alongside the activities of the Polish police: the blackmail of Jews. It was open to all Polish connoisseurs of ineffably Jewish elements in physiognomy; perhaps ears were a trifle too large or too well articulated, or eyelids were heavier than was becoming to a purebred Slav. The blackmailers' appreciation of the purity of accent and diction was equally fine. Although they often spoke themselves like true children of the slums, they could hear in the speech of a former eminent lawyer or professor of classics the unmistakable gay or sad little tune from the shtetl. If there was no money left to pay off the extortionist one more time, a woman could perhaps try to browbeat him. She might say she was a Sarmatian tracing her descent from unsullied generations of other Sarmatians, all of whose names ended like her own in the noble "ski" of Sobieski and Poniatowski; let him prove the contrary. Sometimes this worked. But with men, there was no cheating, no place for Jewish ruses. Very early in the process would come the simple, logical invitation: If Pan is not a kike, a *żydł-ak*, would he please let down his trousers? A thousand excuses if we are wrong.

Therefore, the attention of Tania now became focused on my circumcised penis; in the new life stretching before us, it was for grandfather and me the mark of Cain oddly placed on the body of Abel. Tania thought that he and I had a good chance of deceiving these keen judges of Jewish traits but only down to the waist. My grandfather, with his old man's flabby skin, might even pass the trousers test if he was careful. It was possible, with surgical glue, to shape and fasten enough skin around the gland to imitate a real uncut foreskin. Grandfather was duly equipped with such glue. On a boy or young man, it would not work; should reconstructive surgery be tried? A consultation was arranged with a Jewish surgeon from Lwów, now living in T., who had left Lwów just before the establishment of the ghetto. The surgeon was unenthusiastic. He had, indeed, performed several operations of this sort. It could be done with grafts. The two basic risks were that the graft would not take and infection. In addition, for a child of my age, there was the problem of growth. My penis would become longer but the grafted skin would not keep pace. I would have trouble with erections. This last consideration tipped the scales. They decided to leave me as I was.

While we were so occupied, a sort of quiet descended on T. There was less food for Jews and Poles alike. On the other hand, the roundups stopped. We received, in care of Reinhard, a letter from grandfather. He had found a place to live in the Mokotów section of Warsaw; we were not to worry. We answered, poste restante, in circumspect terms. The Kramer parents hardly ever went to their shop anymore; there were no buyers. Tania had become their only real source of food. This did not make them more friendly toward her, but they sat in the kitchen with grandmother all day. Irena and I read and played in Tania's room. The coal stove was lit only in the evening; it was extremely cold. We were told to read under the covers on the couch. Irena now allowed me to touch her between the legs; sometimes, she put her legs around my waist and rubbed until her squaw face turned red. We talked about what the Germans would do when they took us away. We did not want to be beaten; Bern had told me that they always beat people before killing them or else they let the Polish police do it for them. They even beat the women they were taking to brothels. A good way out was to insult a German: for instance, spit in an officer's face. Then he would shoot you on the spot. We were not sure that we would get an opportunity to do that. In the roundups, the Germans usually stood off at the side while the others did the work. One could also take poison, but we didn't have any. I knew that Tania was trying to get some for us, but that was a secret. I didn't tell Irena.

Tania was spending very few nights at home now. She would drop in unexpectedly, around midday. They would give her permission to leave the office to see her sick mother. She told us that Erika, Reinhard's daughter, had arrived. She was eighteen, very nice but badly dressed, like a real German. Reinhard got the second apartment; it had belonged to Jews. They were fixing it in the evening, after Tania's office closed. She said that every time Reinhard brought china or crystal for the apartment she had to laugh inside; she was wondering if it would turn out to be our own. Reinhard and she had to be very careful not to let their friendship be noticed. Nobody minded if he simply protected her, her work was so good; but having an affair with a Jewish woman was punished by death.

Late one afternoon Tania arrived pale and out of breath. Grandmother and I were sitting in the kitchen with the Kramers. Tania had no food with her, she was not taking off her coat and she did not sit down. She just stood there, staring at my grandmother and looking uncomfortable. I thought that perhaps something had happened to grandfather and asked if she could come with me to our room; I wanted to show her something. She followed me, quickly closed the door behind us, said I was at last becoming intelligent, and sent me back to the kitchen to get grandmother. As soon as we were together, she told us in whispers that the next morning, before dawn, all Jews in T. would be taken away. Reinhard had just found out; we were to keep this to ourselves or we would all be dead. She would go back to the kitchen in a moment, act as normal as she could, and then say good-night and leave for the office. We must remain very quiet, no packing, just take grandmother's jewelry, her fur coat and my warm coat, and be downstairs at the entranceway at eight sharp, like the evening grandfather left. Reinhard would come for us; she would try to be with him. Then she kissed us, said not to be afraid and was gone.

We ate a silent supper with the Kramers. Grandmother complained that she was feeling her liver again. She would lie down in her room and rest. She wanted me with her; I could play with Irena another time. Once

out of the kitchen, we got our things together. Grandmother turned out the light. A few minutes before eight,
we went through the corridor of the apartment—my
grandmother saying, Help me, please, to the toilets—
and then, as quickly as she could manage it, we stum-
bled in the dark along the balcony and down to the gate.
The car was there, with Tania.

Reinhard's apartment was on the ground floor in a
building less than a kilometer away. The curtains were
tightly drawn; all the lights were on. I had become
unaccustomed to so much light; our electricity was
always being cut. In the dining room, there was a
chandelier, and the sideboard and various little tables
were crowded with porcelain figurines and lamps of
various sizes with tassels hanging from their shades.
For the first time, I could take a good look at Reinhard. He was bald. I had expected his sleeve to be
empty, but he seemed to have two arms. Then I noticed that on his left hand he wore a glove and that
he used that hand only to push with. Fruit, cakes and
sausages were set out on the dining-room table. Erika
appeared carrying a teapot. She and Tania were making a lot of noise, asking my grandmother if she was
comfortable and telling her to have some of the ham
that Tania presented in a little dish—it had no fat, it
was perfectly safe for her. Reinhard leaned back in
his chair. He had unbuttoned his jacket. I saw that
he wore white suspenders. He motioned for me to sit
down next to him and said we had the same important
woman in our lives. My aunt was very beautiful and
very good. We would drink *Brüderschaft*. He filled
his glass, told me it was cognac and I could have a
little too to put me back in the saddle after the ad-
ventures of the evening. Then he showed me how to
hook my arm with his good arm, look deep into his

eyes and gulp the drink down. In no time, my German would be as good as Tania's, he assured me. He would put Erika in charge.

Soon it was time for sleep. Tania said that for that night they would make up a bed for me on the dining-room sofa; later they would get a cot, so I could be with Erika. As I had no pajamas, it was all right to stay in my clothes. She kissed me and said I had been polite; she was proud of me.

I think I fell asleep the moment she left; I had no dreams. But almost as abruptly, I was awake again. Tania and Reinhard were in the room, talking in loud whispers. Then Reinhard went out, and I heard Tania crying harder than I had ever heard before. I got up from the sofa and went to her. She was standing at the window, the curtain parted so that she could see out and yet remain hidden. I stood beside her, and she knelt down and put her arms around me. We were looking out on the long avenue that cut T. in two, leading directly to the railroad station. The sky was already turning gray. Here and there a streetlamp was burning. In that uncertain light, we saw the Jews of T. marching to their train in a long, disorderly procession. They carried suitcases and bundles; even children had packages. They must have been given time to pack. A great many Germans were on the sidewalks. Polish police hurried people along. There were no Jewish militiamen with them. Tania whispered that that was because they were also being marched to the station. We were close to the people on the street, at our ground-floor window, but I heard absolutely no sounds. I tried to look for the Kramers and Irena, but there were so many and it was so hard to distinguish faces that I never saw them. After perhaps an hour, the avenue

was empty. They must have all reached the station.
Reinhard was right. By Christmas of 1941, T. had become *judenrein*.

III

THE DOOR BETWEEN TANIA AND REINHARD'S ROOM
and mine was opened just a crack, letting in light and
the sound of the Wehrmacht radio's last bulletin for the
day. It was a woman's voice, lively and confident.
The developments again were favorable for the Reich;
the newscaster passed in review the positions of troops
from Africa to the eastern front, paying homage to the
steadfastness with which Germany's soldiers bore the
cold and snow in the empty Russian steppes. At every
evening at eleven, she played "Lili Marlene" and, going off the air, wished us a good night. We were in
Lwów. The open door was a concession of Reinhard's.
Erika had gone back to Bremen; I was afraid to be
alone; the open door was better in the end than having
Tania get up each time I began to sob. Still, this sort
of yielding to my caprices or nerves was against good
principles of education, and Reinhard liked to justify it
each time by the benefit I derived from the radio. Listening was good for my German and for my general
understanding of the world situation.

I liked the songs on the radio. They were about soldiers and the girls waiting for them or welcoming them
home. Erika had taught me the words to many of them;
we used to sing them together. My favorite, which we
heard almost as often as "Lili Marlene," was about a
soldier keeping watch alone in a wintry field. He thinks

of Anna and his luck: soon it will be time to go home. He has been through much dirt and rubbish, but all of that will soon disappear. Then came the refrain known, so the song assured us, to every private and lieutenant: Everything will pass, everything will go by, but those who love each other will forever be true.

I tried to apply this notion to myself. It was clear that I loved Tania and my grandparents and, of course, my father, although he had left me behind and might be dead anyway. This would not change; we would remain true. I was close to loving Erika. I was not sure anymore about Zosia and preferred not to think about her. On the other hand, it was hard to imagine how the dirt and rubbish would disappear. The war would surely end someday, but what would happen then? Reinhard was convinced that Germany would win; it was winning. The occasional retreats of the Wehrmacht near Moscow, usually followed by advances, were just the hunter's skill deployed against a dying bear; none of the other powers, not even England, could resist German hardness. I felt he was right. German soldiers were better. Nothing would stand in the way of their tanks and guns. But, in that case, were we not a part of the rubbish that had to disappear, perhaps even should disappear, for the sake of the future? How would that be accomplished? I put these questions to Tania. She would shake her head and say that nobody had ever defeated Russia or England; we just had to stay alive long enough. Deep in my heart, I did not believe her. The soldiers who were being routed on every front would not suddenly stop being inferior and weak. Besides, even if the war were to end without Germany ruling the whole world, I did not see how we could be rescued. The Gestapo would never allow us to walk out free from the apartment Reinhard had given us in Lwów, so

that we could board some train for London or New
York. The Germans would kill us as soon as they found
out what Reinhard had done.

I missed Erika. She was a part of the future, even if
the rest of us—Tania, grandfather, grandmother and I—
were not. When we were still in T., she had told me
about Germany and how strong Germany was. She was
not in the Hitlerjugend, because she didn't like meet-
ings and marching around. Her uncle and aunt wanted
her to join, but Reinhard didn't care. Just like everyone
else, though, she had done national service. It was required of girls and boys, first during summer vacations
and then, for at least one year, full time. She had already finished her term in the countryside. She had
worked on a farm. She learned to milk cows, to mow
and bale hay and to work a harvester. They drilled just
like soldiers. It was glorious. At night, they slept in
large, airy barns, one for the boys and one for the girls,
but if a boy wanted to take a girl into a haystack, he
could. The life was healthy. She showed me how strong
she had become: her breasts and the muscles in her
arms and thighs were all hard. She could wrestle Reinhard's good arm down anytime. The people of his gen-
eration had spent too much time in beer halls. That was
why everything about them was so complicated.

She lived in Bremen with her aunt and uncle. Her
aunt was her mother's sister. She had been with them
since her mother died, when she was a baby. That is
what made her and me alike, two orphans, brother and
sister souls. She thought her aunt liked Reinhard better
than her husband. The apartment in Bremen was very
small, nothing like this Jewish apartment in T. When
Reinhard came to visit during her school vacations, he
had to sleep with Erika in her bed, since there was no
spare bed. Her aunt would get into their bed in the

morning, as soon as the uncle went to work, and they would all joke together. The aunt would do anything to get close to Reinhard. My aunt was different, she and my grandmother were refined; they were ladies; one could learn from them every day. She didn't care about Reinhard and my aunt; at least Tania wasn't her mother's sister. So far as she was concerned, it wasn't our fault we were Jews. There used to be nice Jews in Bremen, like the ones Reinhard had worked for before he moved to Essen. Those Jews had gone to England. It was too bad we had not gone to England, although probably it didn't matter. The German army would soon be there as well. She hoped Reinhard could keep us without getting into hot water.

We knew that she would have to go back to Bremen and report for her factory assignment. Production was more important now than studies; even Reinhard thought so. She planned to come back to see us in T. on her first holiday in the summer unless, by then, the war was over. In that case, Reinhard should return to his old job in Essen. They would not need a manager with his experience in a place like T. after the Russians had been beaten. She wondered where we would be once he left. That was a puzzle to which we could never find an answer, and whenever we talked about it, I could see that Erika did not really have much hope of Reinhard keeping us or of our being in some way a part of the future.

Erika's impending departure created another puzzle, which Reinhard and Tania apparently had not anticipated. After she left, how would he explain the evidence of life in her apartment? Even if all three of us were to move to his apartment, which he did not wish because it was too small, what was he to do about his Polish cleaning woman, the supplies of food out of scale

with a bachelor's existence, voices that might be over-
heard? There were long consultations between him and
Tania, usually in their room, but sometimes also with
grandmother, while Erika and I played gin rummy. I
was reading *Treasure Island* in Polish. Long John Silver's pursuit of Jim terrified me. It was bound to end
badly. Erika didn't know the story; Reinhard was the
only person in her family who liked books. We decided
I would read aloud to her, trying to translate into German. I could skip hard and boring passages. That gave
Erika another opportunity to work on my German,
about which Reinhard seemed to care more and more.
The consultations stalled. Reinhard asked Erika to stay
until he sorted things out. She was glad to do it if it
was not too long. She was happy in T.; we were nicer
than her real family, but she didn't want trouble.

When they finally did sort things out, no one was
happy. Once again, we were breaking the promise that
we would stay together, but it had to be. Reinhard decided that he would keep grandmother with him in T.
He would be less lonely that way, and she was so quiet
and needed so much rest that her presence would not
be noticed. He would simply forbid the cleaning woman
to open the door to her room: military secrets inside it.
You peek, you are shot. When the woman was gone,
grandmother could do as she liked; they would have
their evening meal together. She would make *zrazy* and
naleśniki for him, and they would have private feasts.
But Tania and I were going to Lwów, where he had an
apartment ready for us. We would use the Aryan papers
grandfather had gotten for us. It was better than going
to Warsaw because, if we were so near, he could be
with us at least once a week. We would have to be
careful about going out because there were people in
Lwów who might recognize Tania. From that point of

view only, Warsaw was preferable. When grandmother felt better, and we had gotten used to Lwów, she would join us. It was all temporary and had to be done immediately while Erika was still there, and Erika had to be in Bremen in less than a week. We did as he said. Just as the Germans were losing the battle of Moscow, we said good-bye to grandmother and left for Lwów.

Tania and I began our life there in another former Jewish apartment, full of mirrors and carpets, which Reinhard had arranged to have unsealed. The mezuzah was still at the side of the front door. Most of the clothes of the previous owners were gone; otherwise, it was as if they had left very neatly, though in a hurry. Their name was inside book covers. They were not people Tania knew; she said that made it easier. I found a collection of lead soldiers and artillery pieces, better and more complete than the one I had in our old house in T. It must have belonged to an older boy. I decided that all these troops were the Wehrmacht and SS; they looked like winners. My old soldiers were more like the tattered Russian army that had let itself be chased from T. all the way to Moscow in six months.

Directly after "Lili Marlene," Reinhard would turn off the radio. He and Tania would lie in bed talking and laughing for a while. My lamp was out, but I had trouble sleeping. Reinhard said it was natural; I went out so little. I would watch the thin wedge of light from their room on the floor and listen. I was jealous of Reinhard. It seemed to me that Tania had never been more beautiful. Her face was pensive and soft. She was wearing her hair very long. She said this was the style of her new hairdresser, Monsieur Guerre. Perhaps because it was so long, her hair seemed darker, the color of chestnuts after they have been polished in one's hand.

She had very few dresses and saved them for Reinhard's visits. When we were alone in the apartment, she wore peignoirs and matching mules. She laughed that Reinhard was better at supplying lingerie than dresses or skirts: that was all right, she didn't mind looking the kept woman with me. But, just to tease him, she invariably received him in a dress or skirt and sweater and took her time about changing into the lacy garments he preferred. She said this was all she could afford right then by way of a revolt of slaves. At last, their light would go out. I would lie in my bed quietly until they and I fell asleep.

We had no maid. One could not know how nosy she would be or what tales she might tell. Tania shopped for food first thing in the morning. She would hurry, to reduce the chances of being recognized and the time we were separated. We never went out with Reinhard; a German officer with a Polish woman and child would attract too much attention. As it was, Tania thought everyone in the building, beginning with the janitress, was giving her the evil eye, which she said was a very good thing: let them mutter about the German's tart and her bastard, it will keep their minds off the Jewish question.

My walks with Tania were in the evening, progressively later as the days grew longer, for we did not want to go out before nightfall. We would stride rapidly down streets lit by sparse lamps and an occasional shop window. So long as the cold weather lasted, Tania was delighted. She claimed that these were perfect conditions. All our Aryan friends were at dinner or playing cards; no time to hunt the polluting Jew. The city belonged to the underworld, old and new. I suffered from her jokes. I thought they made us feel even lonelier. I didn't like the thought of being a criminal. Besides, if we were

criminals, like the pirates in *Treasure Island*, we should
be getting some profit from it. But we didn't; we were
always afraid and nobody was afraid of us.

Spring came, and Tania and I were no longer solitary
figures rushing and slipping on the frozen, dirty snow
that nobody bothered to shovel off the sidewalks. We
had to pay more attention. Tania's technique for avoiding recognition changed. We were now to walk slowly
and nonchalantly; that attracted the least attention. She
would wear a toque with a little voilette. My feeling of
shame during these expeditions was intense. Reinhard
had gotten clothes for me at the Wehrmacht store. They
were very new, a little too large, and had a shape that
had nothing to do with my body. I thought I looked
different from all other boys, like a funny box on two
legs. My shoes, which laced over the ankles, were a
separate center of shame. Somehow, there was a short-
age of long shoelaces in T. and Lwów that even Reinhard could not overcome. As a result, I had to tie my
shoes with laces that had been broken in many places
and tied together, and I could either wear my shoes
laced only to the middle, which I thought made me look
like a beggar, or I could lace them to the top after a
struggle with the hideous knots that took forever to push
through the eyelets. I knew that everyone saw these
knots; they showed I was an outcast.

Tania talked to me now a great deal, and not just
about manners or to scold. She wanted me to understand about Reinhard. It was very important that I be
affectionate when he came to see us. He was a good,
simple man. He liked, above all, to have a good time,
but he had got into a situation where the only good time
he had was with her. She hoped she could make that
be enough. When she began, it was just to make things
easier in T.; she had not yet realized Reinhard would

save us. Now she thought she loved him, probably as much as she had ever loved anybody. It was hard to make comparisons: she claimed she had always had a heart of stone except when it came to grandfather and me, and neither of us even knew she loved him. In the beginning of her life with my father and me in T., she had thought that she might get to love my father or anyway to make him fall in love, but she found that he measured everything out with an eyedropper—time, affection, money. He had been a perfect match for my mother who took after grandmother and had done nothing very right or very wrong in her short life. After a while, she, Tania, settled for being the perfect aunt, with only Bern sometimes there to remind her that one could have fun. But the war had opened for her an even grander career. She could be the perfect, selfless aunt who became a courtesan to save her little nephew, a sort of small-town, small-scale Esther.

We began to be more regular about lessons. Tania didn't want me to go on making mistakes in German. It embarrassed her to have Reinhard correct me. We could not speak German on our walks, but we promised to speak nothing else at home, except when we were working on other subjects. Tania didn't like arithmetic; she pretended she had forgotten the multiplication table. I could do the exercises in the book by myself and keep them for Reinhard to review. He was good at it, and it was good policy to have him explain things to me. She had also forgotten geography. But Tania knew and loved Polish literature and, especially, Polish poetry. She thought declamation was at the center of understanding; only if one spoke a poem could its value be revealed, and even then only if the verse was spoken well. She also believed that poetry had to be revisited often. Therefore, poems should be memorized. If one really knew a poem by heart, one could recite, barely moving one's lips, like a priest reading his breviary, as one walked about, or got dressed, or waited to fall asleep. It would fill unused voids in one's mind.

Tania especially admired Mickiewicz, for style and content. She decided we would read his medieval epic, *Konrad Wallenrod*; the subject was subversive, made for us. I soon saw why. Konrad has recently become the all-powerful master of the Teutonic Knights who have conquered all of East Prussia and are threatening the destruction and enslavement of pagan Lithuania. The time has come for a final onslaught against the Lithuanians. The knights are impatient and seemingly invincible; nothing can prevent the victory of the Germans and the cross. But Konrad, like us, is a fraud: his name is not Wallenrod; he is not German; he is Lithuanian. The knights kidnapped him when he was a child and brought him up as their own, and now he will betray them. He will so bungle the campaign that the Order will be mortally wounded, the knights humiliated, and Lithuania saved. Of course, some of the knights will puzzle out the truth and kill Konrad, but he will die happily, like Samson, because he has avenged his people.

Alas, the Wehrmacht radio was reporting nothing as threatening for the Reich. German troops had reached the Caucasus and entered Stalingrad. They were on the Volga. Africa was far away and irrelevant to Europe; each English success there seemed followed by a defeat. The Americans were bleeding to death on the atolls of the Pacific. Without any mention on the radio, the ghetto in Lwów had been emptied. Reinhard began to speak of concentration camps where people were meant to die. We wondered if we were the only Jews left in Lwów.

Reinhard was worried about my grandmother. Both he and she thought she had jaundice. She was very tired and very uncomfortable. All the remedies suggested by Tania, the repository of my father's science, had been tried; a doctor was needed but Reinhard didn't want to put himself in the hands of the Catholic surgeon in T. Perhaps, if grandmother improved even a little, he could bring her to Lwów. He was also worried about Bern. A personage he had never seen before—he did not even know if the man was a Jew or a Pole, perhaps just an agent provocateur—had come to the apartment with a message that Bern and his friends were in desperate need: Could he, Reinhard, help? He threw the man out, but the event could not be ignored. It could only mean that Bern had talked. If he had talked, that meant there were others who could talk in turn. If only he could emigrate to Palestine with us! This became his favorite joke.

That there were other Jews in Lwów became evident shortly afterward, during one of Tania's and my evening walks. A man approached us and began talking very quickly, asking Tania not to be frightened and above all not to appear frightened. He had something of interest to relate. Tania's face looked frozen and her grip on my hand tightened; we had been told that this was the usual approach of a street blackmailer of Jews. This man, however, pretended to be different. He knew Bern. He knew my father. He had often seen Tania in the past, although she did not remember him. He was himself a Jew, trying to survive in Lwów, like ourselves. Could Tania give him some money? God would reward her and her little nephew; he had Aryan papers that cost a fortune, he was paying his former janitor to hide his wife, there was almost nothing left. Unfortunately, his wife did not have the right look; she could not pass using Aryan papers. Tania said we had become poor as well, but she would do what she could. She would leave an envelope for him if he suggested a spot; it would be there tomorrow. They settled on the space behind a plaster figure in the entrance of the post office. Hertz— he asked us to call him by his real name—commended Tania for her prudence. Panna is right not to want to meet me, I could be followed; then all three of us birds would be caught in one net. But Panna must not worry that we will lose contact. I have noted where she and the precious boy reside.

We said good-bye. Tania turned the corner, and then another, until she found a street bench. We sat down. She put my hand on her breast to show me how hard her heart was beating. She said we were trapped; it did not matter that this man was a Jew. He reeked of vulgarity and swinishness. He would bleed us white and then sell us. We should immediately move to another apartment, perhaps out of Lwów, but she did not dare tell Reinhard. Coming on top of the messenger from Bern, it would be the last straw. She would give the man money, not too much but not too little. If she gave too little he would be back right away, and we had to play for time. She would put the envelope in the agreed place this very evening. She did not want him to be able to see her depositing it tomorrow; he might be waiting somewhere near the post office, hoping to show her to another bandit. She took me by the hand and walked home so fast that I almost had to run to keep up. Her night-table drawer was full of bank notes. She counted out a thin pile, then put some back, looked for an envelope and added some more money before licking the envelope sealed. We went to the post office at the same mad pace, but taking a roundabout route. Every once in a while, Tania would stop at a store win-

dow to look at something or to straighten her coat. I
realized she was studying the street behind her. But we
were not being followed.

After she had put the envelope behind the sculpture
we went home, this time very slowly. We sat down in
the kitchen. Tania made hot chocolate for both of us.
She was crying. She said we were all alone; she could
not telephone Reinhard, she could not telephone grandfather, there were three days to Saturday, when Reinhard would come, grandfather should not have left us
all alone. Then she told me that the worst was that she
herself had sunk morally to the level of the lowest of
blackmailers; my grandfather would be ashamed of her.
This man Hertz was surely just a poor Jew, trying to
survive and to save his wife's life. And she was so
afraid, so degraded, that she had no trust left and no
pity. It was she whom Hertz and every decent man
should flee.

*Pity is no stranger to hell. Hell brims over with self-
pity. The case of the vulgar damned, outside the pre-
cincts of the enameled green,* verde smalto, *where
congregate the biblical and intellectual elite, is clear-
cut. They wail and gnash their teeth as they suffer the
ghoulish punishments devised by supreme wisdom,*
somma sapienza, *working hand in hand with primal
love,* primo amore. *Sometimes they feel they have been
entrapped: if only one had forborne from giving that
last bit of evil counsel or had repented earlier, eternity
would not be filled with the same unbearable pain,
guaranteed to augment when, after the Last Judgment,
the flesh shall be rejoined with the spirit. The self-pity
of Dante and his Mantuan guide is more interesting.*

Virgil, like his colleagues of the verde smalto, *with
slow-moving and grave eyes,* con occhi tardi e gravi,

resembles a Jew with technical qualifications indispensable to the Reich; no Barbariccia or other devil will sink a fork into his rump; not for him the cesspool of the Malebolge. Comparing his situation with that of the other damned, he might consider himself pretty lucky. But not in the least—at the mere thought of it he turns pale, tutto smorto; his problem is that he and his colleagues live without hope in desire, sanza speme vivemo in disio.

Dante's capacity for self-pity is equally colossal, although he enjoys highest-level protection. Early on, he learns on unimpeachable authority that he is only a tourist in Inferno and does not need to come back. Just in case the reader missed it, the point is made over and over again. Yet Dante never stops complaining. He alone endures the fatigue of the monstrous journey; he is undone by the stench and stunned by the local light and noise effects; he sorrows over the prediction of his future exile.

Pity for others who are suffering in hell is generally repressed: when Dante sees the sorcerers march backward through their valley, because their faces, twisted to look over the loins, deny them the power of seeing forward, he weeps at the vision of our image so contorted. The hem of self-pity is showing. Virgil immediately administers a tongue-lashing. Who is more wicked than he that sorrows at God's judgment? Pity for the rich and famous, although analytically no more defensible, is apt to escape censure: witness the treatment of Brunetto Latini, Farinata and Ulysses, among others. In this manner tenderhearted anti-Semites will find infinitely more pitiful the indignities or, worse yet, financial ruin suffered by a Jewish member of the upper set than the death of some little furrier from Tarnopol who was shot and then shoved into a common grave he had *helped to dig. Dante's rejoicing when he sees the hap-less Filippo Argenti drowning in mud is such that Virgil cannot contain himself. Blessed is the mother, he exclaims, that bore this virtuously indignant son.*

But poetry has its own power, and a poet's words overcome even the hardness of his own heart. In that place mute of all light, as the two poets trudge on, setting their feet on the emptiness of sufferers that seems like real bodies, sopra lor vanità che par persona, *one question reverberates louder than all others: Who piles on these travails and pains, and why does our guilt waste us so?* Perché nostra colpa sì ne scipa?

On Friday, the next morning, I was in our kitchen. It was a large, bright room, painted white, with a square table in the middle. The stove, like all kitchen stoves in Poland at that time, was a black, iron box, itself not unlike a table, fired by coal. Getting it started properly with kindling, creating zones of differing degrees of heat, and then keeping the fire going from breakfast through the day were skills cooks were proud of. Tania had asked the cook in T. to teach her before the servants were let go. Now she taught me in turn. I loved lighting the stove and preparing our coffee, which was real, not ersatz. I would set the milk on the cooler part of the plaque, so that it would not boil over; cleaning burnt milk from the iron stove top to Tania's satisfaction was not easy. I also had a hot area, on which I made toast. My special invention, of which Tania approved, was soft-boiled eggs cooked without a timer. I discovered that the equivalent of a four-minute egg could be produced, without failure, by putting eggs into cold water, bringing the water to a boil and withdrawing the eggs immediately. Tania liked breakfast in bed. When Reinhard wasn't there, I would get it all ready and arrange it on a tray large enough for two. We would then eat it in her bed, side by side.

I was about to take the milk off the fire when I saw, making his way with great speed down to the kindling box beside the stove, a huge spider, suspended by the thread it was producing. It was the largest I had seen, with knobbly legs he kept folding and unfolding. I had a dish towel in my hand to grasp the milk pan, but instead I reached for the spider with it. He scurried up to get out of my way, but I was faster. I squashed him against the wall. When I took the towel away, I saw that I had made a black-and-red spot. Also, the milk had boiled over and was spreading across the stove. I quickly rescued the pan, refilled it, and was beginning to clean up when Tania came into the kitchen. She had smelled the burnt milk and asked how her chef had gotten into such trouble. Her face was fresh and pink from bed; she put her arms around me. I told her about the spider. She looked at the stain and said very quietly that it was too bad, seeing a spider on Friday was bad luck; killing the spider made bad luck certain.

For my birthday Reinhard had given me a set for making lead soldiers. It consisted of three split iron molds—one for foot soldiers, one for cavalrymen and one for horses—a little pan with a beak for melting lead, and paints and brushes. I would set up the molds on the kitchen table, melt the lead on the stove, pour it into the molds and then quickly plunge the blocks into a pan of cold water. After a few minutes, I could open the molds, and the soldiers or horses would be ready to paint. I used the set to make soldiers from new lead and also to recast broken or worn-out men. After breakfast, I decided to cast a whole new regiment that I would paint white, as camouflage for fighting in the snow. When Reinhard arrived the next day, we would set up the battle at Stalingrad. I had so many lead soldiers now that I could field both armies; before I had used cardboard cutouts for the Russians and the English. Lead soldiers made the battlefield clearer. The field gun Reinhard had also given me worked better against them. It had a spring that pulled back and shot dry peas hard enough to knock over a whole row of soldiers.

The weather was very beautiful that day, sunny with no autumn frost yet in the air. Tania came home from shopping and said it was a pity not to go for a walk until the evening, but we should not break rules. The nicer the day, the more people would be out who might recognize us. But she would go out alone to pass by the post office; she wanted to see if the envelope was gone. She returned perplexed: it was still there.

On our evening walk, we went first to the post office. This time, the envelope was gone. Tania said she was puzzled by her own curiosity; of course, Hertz took the money and couldn't be expected to leave a thank-you note. We walked longer than usual, more slowly than usual, really looking at shop windows, and not just pretending so that Tania could study the street behind us. Tania said that probably this was the period of Jewish holidays; it was odd not to know on what day they began. She asked if I remembered my grandparents' visits to T. and how grandfather was never too tired, never too dressed up to race with me on all fours or gallop around in the garden. Neither she nor my mother nor my uncle had played with him that way. She was sorry that he had never taken me to the synagogue; in better-ordered families boys even younger than I went on the holy days and sat with the men. Now I would never get to hear the ram's horn blown for the New Year. It was the moment in the synagogue my grandfather most looked forward to. It meant that the service was almost over, and he would be able to take off his homburg and light a cigarette. All that was lost. But she would teach me what every Jew must do when his death is near: cover his head, with only his hands if necessary, and say in a loud voice, *Shema Yisrael, Adonai elocheinu, Adonai echad.* Hear, O Israel, the Lord thy God, the Lord is one. That was a way for a Jew not to die alone, to join his death to all those that had come before and were still to come.

The next morning we expected Reinhard around nine as usual. He always left T. early to have a full Saturday with Tania, but it was nearly eleven and he had not yet arrived. Tania said she was worried, but there was nothing to be done: telephoning from the post office was unthinkable. If Reinhard had left, grandmother would not answer. If he was still there, he must have a good reason, and the telephone might ring at an awkward moment. The only thing to do was to wait patiently. She would shop later.

The day wore on uneasily; such a thing had never happened before. She decided we would work on our Mickiewicz. I asked to do my new favorite, a poem about the young colonel of a band of Polish fusiliers fighting against the Russians. He is mortally wounded; the soldiers carry him to a humble forester's hut. Time has come to bid farewell to his horse, belt, saber and saddle. The priest arrives with the last sacraments; peasants crowd to see the hero laid out on a rustic couch. Suddenly, the scales fall from their eyes: this beautiful face, this breast, are not a man's. The colonel is a Lithuanian virgin! Reciting the word "breast" in front of Tania made me blush. I did not want to think about her the way I thought about Zosia and Irena, though I could not always help it. I longed to see or, better yet, touch her breast directly, not through her blouse, as when she wanted me to feel her heart hammer. It occurred to me that Reinhard would not come to Lwów that day. In that case, perhaps she would allow me to sleep in her bed. Then I could put my arms around her and pretend that she was the virgin hero and her breast was in my hand.

Our lesson was interrupted by a persistent ringing of the doorbell. It could not be Reinhard; he had a key. No one, except the janitress, when she came for the garbage, rang our bell. This was not her usual hour. This was danger. Tania said: Go into your room, shut the door and stay there, I was right about Hertz from the start. I heard her steps, rapid and sharp, then the front door opening, then a loud gasp and the door slamming shut. She was crying and speaking Polish. It was not the Gestapo. I opened my door just wide enough to see and hear Hertz. He was saying Panna Taniu, Panna Taniu, this is not the time to cry, this is the time to be brave and very quick. Please trust me, you have no choice, please let me help. But Tania was crying harder and harder, then she was kneeling on the floor and hitting it with her fists, and saying, I don't want help, I want it all to end now, take the boy away, I will give you all my money, just leave me here. Hertz kept on talking and quieting her. Slowly, I understood his story.

There was a network of the underground, mostly Jewish, in touch with Jewish partisans in the forest. He was in some way a part of it. That was how he got news, sometimes from the forest and in this case from T. Bern and the men with whom he went to the forest had been unlucky; they had wandered about, unable to find the Jewish group they intended to join. They did make contact with Polish partisans, who wanted no part of them. Some Polish units were very anti-Semitic; they preferred to have Jewish partisans fall into the hands of the Wehrmacht. In the end, Bern and his friends did little more in the forest than hide and raid neighboring farms to get food. The peasants got tired of it and helped the Germans set a trap. When they came to the usual village a few days ago, soldiers were waiting in every hut. Several partisans, including Bern, were taken alive. The Germans must have worked on them until they talked. Anyway, at dawn this morning, the Gestapo had gone to Reinhard's apartment. They broke the door, but he was too fast for them. By the time they found him, he had already shot the old lady and then, right before them, sat down next to her on the bed and blew the top off his own head. A Polish policeman who was with them transmitted the story. So there was no immediate danger for Panna Tania and the boy; no one who knew how to find Panna Tania was left alive in T.

All the same, Hertz thought we should leave the apartment the next day at the latest. The Gestapo might find clues when they looked in Reinhard's papers. It was also better, for the same reason, to get new Aryan papers with different names and leave for Warsaw. One could disappear in Warsaw better than in Lwów. He asked to see our papers. They were not bad, he concluded, but if Tania could pay he would get something really excellent, real papers and not forgeries, for a mother and son. In his judgment it was a mistake for Tania to present herself as my aunt. The idea of a young aunt living alone with a nine-year-old nephew could only arouse suspicion. Was she not a Jewess who had been unable to get papers for a mother and son and invented the aunt story? It was better to be a widow with a child or, best of all, someone whose husband retreated east with the Polish army and was now either dead or in a Russian prison camp for officers. That story was good for use with Poles and Germans. It was more complicated than saying her husband was in a prison camp in Germany, but a husband in a German camp could lead to problems with the German police.

Tania had become extremely calm. She took Hertz's hand and kissed it; she said she had to thank him for more than he realized. We would do exactly as he advised, except that she wanted to leave the apartment that very day. The janitress was never there on Saturday afternoons. She and I would slip out with a small suitcase each. Did Hertz know where we could find a temporary place to stay? It turned out he did; there were furnished apartments, very small, in a building that was not very pleasant. They were usually rented to ladies of a special sort. Tania should say to the landlady that she had been given the address at the railroad station buffet. We had just arrived from Sambor; we were on our way to Cracow, but I had a fever, probably the beginning of measles, and she decided to interrupt the journey until the disease declared itself or the fever fell. That would give her a pretext to remain as long as necessary. With this landlady we might as well use the papers we had. But if Tania would meet him the following week at the post office, he hoped to be able to give her the new ones. He thought it was better that he not come to see us. If she was a stranger in Lwów with a sick child, why would she be receiving a visit?

The house we went to on Hertz's advice resembled the one we had lived in with Pan and Pani Kramer in T. It had similar interior balconies, linked by straight stairs, and a wide gateway leading from the street to the yard. There was a well with a pump in the courtyard, but it was a remnant of older times; here, we had running water in the rooms. The apartment the landlady was willing to rent to Tania was off the first balcony, reached directly from the courtyard. It consisted of a kitchen, a little living room with artificial flowers on a table in the corner and a bedroom with a large bed. The toilet flushed, and for bathing there was a brown zinc tub in the kitchen that one could fill with hot water. The windows all gave on the balcony; the entrance was through the kitchen.

Tania had brought some bread and ham for our supper, and soap and coffee. We sat down to eat; it was our first meal since the morning. I was very hungry. When we finished, Tania said that we would go to Warsaw soon and find grandfather. Perhaps we could live with him, but we shouldn't count on it. She and I had to get used to the idea that we were quite alone: Tania and Maciek against the world. This was not an easy lesson to learn, but probably the world would beat it into our heads. Then she said that was enough philosophy for one Saturday evening; the two musketeers needed some rest. She opened the bed. The sheets had been washed; we would not worry about what was underneath.

That was our introduction to bedbugs. Tania felt them first. Suddenly, she sat up in bed and said that something strange was happening; she was itching all over. As soon as she turned on the light, we saw them: oblong red dots scurrying from the sheet to the recess between the bed and the headboard. Other red dots were rushing along the wall, some up to crawl behind the frame of the picture of a stag and dogs, some down to the floorboards. We knew all about fleas. They were omnipresent in Poland; when my father came home from the hospital ward or calls to certain patients, he would undress completely in the examination room and give his clothes to the chambermaid. She would beat them, right outside the kitchen, with the same bat that was used at monthly intervals for whacking away at

carpets until not a mote of dust could be seen to rise.
That was the best way to get fleas out of clothes that
couldn't be washed, short of catching them with one's
fingers. But it took Tania a while to identify and name
these insects that bit but didn't jump. Since they seemed
to dislike the light, we decided to sleep with the light
on. Tania said this was just a comical reminder: we
were reaching the lower depths. If the Germans didn't
get us, lice would be next.

The papers were not ready the following week or the
next. The season changed while we waited in that house,
among its strange tenants and their furtive visitors. Tania went out as little as possible, to buy food, to meet
Hertz and give him money while she accepted his excuses, trying not to be noticed, afraid of leaving me
alone. I did not leave the apartment at all. At last, Hertz
delivered our new papers. Although so much time had
passed, once again he advised Tania to leave the city;
he thought it was impossible that the Gestapo would let
a matter of this sort drop; if somehow they found out
about her, eventually they would look in Lwów. They
surely knew that Reinhard spent Saturdays and Sundays
there. Hertz also brought her a gift, two vials of cyanide. He said it was good to have it. In case of need,
one just bit through the glass, which was thin, and left
the Germans and all other troubles behind.

Our departure was now a matter of precise timing
and preparations. Tania wrote a short and vague letter
to my grandfather, telling him to expect us soon, saying
nothing of what had happened. The photograph of the
woman in Tania's new papers looked sufficiently like
her, except that it showed very short, wavy hair. Tania
went to a hairdresser and had her hair cut and curled.
She bought a black coat for herself and a gray coat and

cap for me. She worried about how to transport our
money and grandmother's jewelry. Hertz told her to be
very careful. There were so many black-market opera-
tors on trains that Polish police and even the Feldgendarmerie frequently went through passengers' handbags
and luggage. She decided she would tape the jewelry
to my stomach and chest and the bank notes and gold
coins to herself. We practiced doing it so that it was all
smooth and would not be noticed if we were only
frisked. The jewelry had to be wrapped in cotton anyway; otherwise it would dig into my skin. In the new
papers, my name was no longer Maciek, and Tania was
no longer Tania; I was to be called Janek. Making sure
we used the new names without fail would also require
practice.

We were ready; there was nothing more that Tania or
Hertz thought we should do. Hertz offered to get our
tickets and give them to Tania at the entrance to the
platform. That cut down the time we would need to
spend at the station. At his suggestion, we were going
to take the night train; Hertz said even the Gestapo had
to sleep. There was nothing left to do except wait for
the afternoon to end. Tania and I sat in the kitchen, in
the bleary March light, and played twenty-one for
matches. Suddenly Tania stood up, drew in her breath,
and pointed out the window to the stairs. Walking up
were two Gestapo men in uniform and a third man in a
belted civilian coat but wearing black britches and high
black boots like the others. Tania put her fingers to her
lips and in a whisper told me to hurry to the bedroom,
leave the door open, and hide behind the door. I was
to listen carefully. If they were taking her away or if
they were going toward the bedroom and she shrieked,
I should immediately take the cyanide. Keep it in your

hand, she said, and keep your hand in your pants pocket.

It took what seemed like a long time before they reached our apartment. I listened to their knocking on other doors off the balcony and to muffled conversations. At last, they knocked on the door to our kitchen. From where I was standing I could hear very well. They were checking Tania's papers, looking around the kitchen. They spoke no Polish; she answered them in brash, broken German, using the familiar *du*. She told them they had startled her; she was deep in her game of solitaire. The man in civilian clothes said they wanted a woman with a little boy. The woman had long hair, down to the shoulders. They showed Tania a photograph. They knew the woman and child lived in the building; the landlady had reported their presence to the Polish police. Tania said they should have come sooner. There was such a woman in the next apartment, where they had knocked without getting an answer. She and the boy moved in months ago. But they both went out; she had seen them on the balcony.

There followed some talk among the men I could not make out, and the civilian asked to see Tania's papers again. This time they looked at them longer, and asked her to come into the light at the door so they could compare her to the photograph they had with them and the photograph in her *Kennkarte*. The civilian asked whether she had a young boy or anyone else living in the apartment. Tania laughed the long laugh she used when she teased people who weren't her friends and said they could look through her small apartment if they were curious. In fact, she was too busy with grown men to have little boys around, and except for the three of them, she was alone. But not for long, a friend was coming; a man, not a woman or a little boy, and he

didn't have long hair. If they wished to wait they could
see for themselves. The Germans also laughed and said
they might indeed come back to surprise her when she
was not expecting company. They talked a moment longer, and then I knew they were leaving: the door
slammed; there were heavy steps on the balcony and
soon on the stairs, going down.

Tania remained in the kitchen until they could no
longer be heard. I had not moved from my place behind
the bedroom door; the vial was still in my hand. Then
suddenly she rushed into the room and said, Hurry, we
are getting out of this house. They will come back to
look for the woman in the apartment next door, they
will talk to the landlady, and if that slut is at home she
will get her chance to turn us in.

IV

TANIA AND I ARRIVED IN WARSAW, WITH OUR MONEY and jewelry still safely adhering to our bodies, on the morning of March 30, 1943. While we slept heavily in a railroad compartment crammed with passengers and bundles, fear mixed with fatigue being the strongest of soporifics, RAF bombs for the second time in three days kept awake the population of Berlin. Later that morning, as we looked for the rooming house near the Central Station that Hertz had recommended, Berliners leaving air-raid shelters and resuming their lives in familiar neighborhoods could discern the face of their city-to-be in bomb craters and behind blackened facades of their houses.

There was a unifying theme in Hertz's repertoire of addresses. We were received by a landlady who seemed astonished that a mother and a child were seeking a room in her establishment. Having been told that there was no mistake, that this was the very house Tania had been referred to by a faithful client of hers from Lwów, the landlady, a certain Pani Jadwiga, agreed to take us on the condition that we stay no longer than a week: this was a place for transients, there were no cooking privileges, we would share the toilet with the ladies down the corridor; it would be better if Tania kept me in our room so I didn't get into people's way. Rent was payable for the week in advance. The room she gave us was somewhat larger than our last bedroom in Lwów, with an ampler bed, two little settees covered with red plush, some red plush straight chairs, and a dirty rug. We left our suitcases there and went to mail a letter to grandfather, asking him to meet us in the main entrance of the Cathedral; we would be there at noon every day, beginning the day after tomorrow, until he was able to come. Tania didn't know Warsaw. It was the only suitable monument she could think of that would do equally well in good weather and in the rain.

We were very hungry, and neither of us wanted to bring food to eat in our room. Tania decided we would go to the Central Station buffet for lunch; our disoriented, out-of-town appearance would not make us conspicuous there, but first we had to buy a street map of Warsaw. We studied it over our meal, Tania saying that we had to figure out the city immediately, so that we could get around without asking directions and attracting attention. Then we walked along a route she had memorized to the Saxon Gardens and sat there for a long time on a bench in the feeble afternoon sun. A woman and a little boy spending an hour or more in the park would not seem unusual. We returned to our rooming house the long way, taking Nowy Świat to Aleje Jerozolimskie. By that time, we were so tired that the vision of the plush settees and the bed seemed cozy; we didn't want to return to the station. There was a butcher nearby and also a bakery. Across the street from the house, we found a *mleczarnia*, where one could buy milk and cheese. We pushed a settee to the table, ate our bread and sausage, drank some milk, at last detached the money and jewelry packages from our bodies, and got into bed. Tania said she wasn't going to look at the sheets; she didn't care what they were like.

We took the street map of Warsaw to bed with us. Tania decided we had to study it during every free moment, segment by segment, until we knew it by heart, like a poem. We would quiz each other, and we were going to start right away, because one always remembers best the things one learns just before going to sleep. When we finished, Tania said that she knew I was sleepy, but there were so many problems to solve that she had to talk. She couldn't bear to think about them in silence. Perhaps grandfather would have all the answers, but even so, we had to think through the problems first for ourselves.

To start with, what were we to do with the jewelry and the gold and all those bank notes? We couldn't wear them glued to us all the time, it was too uncomfortable; people got stopped for document checks, and we might be searched. Getting caught with that hoard meant giving most of it away if it was the Polish police, or being taken to the Gestapo if we were caught by the Germans. On the other hand, how could we leave anything of value in this house or any other rooming house we might move to? There was also the question of how to sell the gold or jewelry once we had spent our cash. She couldn't imagine simply walking into a jewelry shop and putting a couple of rings or a bracelet on the counter. She would be cheated. We needed a reliable crook; that was probably the sort of person grandfather would know. And where would we go when our week here was over? Presumably grandfather would know about that as well. Perhaps we could move in with him. We would need, in any case, a story to explain why she was here with me looking for a place to live. We would use Hertz's idea. For instance: wife of Polish officer, doctor in civilian life, prisoner of war in a Russian camp, rest of the family killed in bombardments in 1939

or perhaps deported to Siberia. But why did we leave
Lwów? It must be that her nerves no longer could stand
Lwów after so many losses. That part of the story, she
felt, would have to be perfected as she told it. She would
see how her audience reacted; she might try it on the
landlady here. And how about me, why didn't I go to
school? That I wouldn't go to school was understood
between Tania and me; one couldn't take my penis
where it might be seen, for instance to urinate in the
common toilet, never mind what vicious games boys
might invent. The reason had to be my delicate, con-
genital heart condition. I would be tutored privately;
that might be an additional reason for coming to Warsaw. Teaching privately was forbidden. It may be that
people willing to take the risk would be easier to find
in Warsaw than in Lwów. We could not carry our questions and answers further. Tania turned out the light.
We would sleep.

Our rest was interrupted by the now-familiar red visitors. These were big-city bedbugs, more active and
more ingenious than their cousins in Lwów. Not content with hustling along the sheet and scurrying up and
down walls, they dropped on the bed and on us from
the ceiling and swarmed over the plush of the settees
and chairs. We even saw them run on the floor, staying
close to the wall. The light Tania turned on restored
order. Pressed against each other, we fell asleep. On
subsequent nights, when we were less tired and more
apprehensive about the insect colonies with which we
shared our space, we went to bed with the light on and
cloth bands tied over our eyes. Tania called it Warsaw
blindman's buff.

The struggle against bedbugs became a leitmotiv of
our days and nights in Warsaw. At Pani Jadwiga's there
was nothing to be done other than to turn the bedbugs'

night into day. Our term there was too short. In subsequent rooming houses, more was at stake, sleepless nights being worse than nightmares, and the combat became more varied. On some nights, of course, too discouraged or overwhelmed by the number and tenacity of the enemy, we lay awake in the lamplight or simply let the bedbugs feed. But in the day, we went on the offensive. Tania sprinkled foul-smelling powders on the mattress, under the mattress, around the walls. We poured boiling water on suspected nests. We exposed the bed, if the space and the location of the window permitted, to the disinfecting rays of the sun. This activity provided, in addition to a temporary material improvement in our comfort, another war game I did not mention to Tania: in this limited sphere, I could be a hunter and an aggressor, like SS units destroying partisans in the forest or, very soon, rebellious Jews in the ghetto of Warsaw. The SS sometimes had to act in secret. So did we. Our landladies resented any mention of bedbugs on their premises; we were in no position to antagonize them. From that point of view, our favorable experience with chemical agents paralleled that of the Reich. They were the easiest means of murder to conceal. Use of boiling water and, at night, manual extermination of fleeing bugs presented considerable risks and difficulties. The former laid us open to the charge of destroying property by spillage of liquids. The latter often left red blood stains on the wallpaper. Stealth and lies were needed to cover our operations with water. We could sometimes, unobserved, rush the pot from the kitchen we shared with the landlady and the other lodgers into our room; at other times Tania claimed she needed to prepare a hot-water bottle. In one room that we rented we worked undisturbed and undetected: we had permission to make tea or coffee on an alcohol stove within the room, and we boiled as much water as we wanted. I was the principal nighttime executioner of escaping bedbugs. Early on, I tired of scraping dried blood off walls and sheets with my fingernails—it was unpleasant and ineffective—yet working with a wet rag often made the stain worse. The technique I eventually perfected protected the walls. I would corner the bug on the wall with a cupped left hand, sweep it to the floor with the right, and trample it to death.

Tania's research, confirmed eventually by my grandfather, led her quickly to conclude that for Jews like us on Aryan papers there was no apparent means of renting an apartment of our own in the capital or, for that matter, in Praga, the suburb on the other side of the Vistula. Perhaps apartments were to be had in Warsaw, possibly even at a price we could afford, but to find one it was necessary to have connections with Poles, and such connections were precisely what we wished to avoid. Therefore, the likes of us were relegated to renting rooms in more or less spacious apartments, usually belonging to more or less elderly ladies of reduced means. These ladies did not necessarily live in shabby buildings; indeed, apartments in buildings below a certain level of petit bourgeois pretension would have been too small to lend themselves to the business. In the apartments we got to know well, a room or two, including perhaps the salon, would be reserved for the landlady, and the other rooms, in some prewar era of greater ease probably intended for children, opening on a long corridor, were at present available to lodgers. Each such room would contain a single bed, sometimes narrow, sometimes quite comfortable (two beds would not have left enough space for other furnishings), a table, a few chairs, a wardrobe, a bookcase, a washstand. At the end of the corridor, there would be, in the best of circumstances, a bathroom with a tub with running water and its own gas or oil heater, used by everyone in the apartment. Next to it would be a separate cubicle containing a toilet, also for communal use. At peak hours, in the morning when the lodgers awoke and after dinner when they prepared for the night, unpleasant questions of priority were apt to arise concerning the toilet. Our policy was to avoid unpleasantness; we made sure to have a chamber pot in our room and could yield politely to those whose needs were urgent.

The landladies of Warsaw's communal apartments did not feed their lodgers. One bought one's own food, kept it in the room as best one could, iceboxes not being in general use, cooked it in the kitchen, and ate it at a common dining-room table or in one's room, depending on the custom of the place and the lodger's degree of dourness. And who were these lodgers? Dreary, unmarried office employees, widows and widowers whose apartments had been destroyed in some bombardment, and the deceivers: Jews with Aryan papers.

My existence continued to be a problem not susceptible to a pleasant solution. Children in these establishments were a rarity; they attracted attention and, therefore, danger. Questions of the sort Tania and I had rehearsed were to be answered before they were asked, so that the inquisitive landlady or fellow lodger would never begin the dreaded inquiry that might lead to the truth: Why did that young woman's family not take her in, rather than let her and her boy lead a solitary, peculiar life in this place? They don't seem poor, otherwise how could she afford the rent that we who work, or we who have a little pension, pay with difficulty? She doesn't work. What kind of pension do young people of her sort have? Could they be Jews? Let's see if we can find out; it's amusing to set a trap.

The days and nights that would teach us these new skills were still to be lived. On the third day after our arrival in Warsaw, we finally saw my grandfather. He was waiting for us at the Cathedral. As always, he was bareheaded; he wore a short black leather overcoat I did not recognize. We embraced, he looked me over, lifted me up for a kiss and said I had grown but was still his little man. Tania put her arm through his and drew us all inside. The Cathedral was nearly empty. We sat down in a pew near a side altar, and she told him what had happened. Grandfather did not cry; he seemed to sink into himself. I saw now how he had changed. Where it was not stained by nicotine, his mustache was as white as his hair; there were folds in the skin on his neck; his shirt collar looked worn and also yellowed as though from smoking. The fingers of his right hand were almost brown; he had probably stopped using a cigarette holder. After a long silence, grandfather said that Reinhard had been a fine man. He hoped that he would have had as much presence of mind himself and as much courage; if grandmother realized what was happening, she surely blessed Reinhard in her last thoughts. He was proud of Tania. The trick was for the three of us to stay alive. With America in the war and the English finally bombing Berlin it made sense to try hard.

He told us that in Mokotów he had a room and the use of the kitchen in an apartment. The landlady was a pleasant old cocotte, he liked her, and in fact the room wasn't bad. But he did not think we could move in with him. For one thing, he doubted that the landlady would agree to giving up another room. More important, the only other lodgers were a young woman about Tania's age and her boy, a little younger than I. He was quite sure they were Jews; the woman had a strange look about her, probably she bleached her hair to make it less red, and there was something too tender about her eyes. He was less sure that they understood about him. Having more Jews than absolutely necessary under one roof made no sense, it multiplied the danger, and this Jewish lady could be a real menace; she acted scatter-brained. He might have moved out on account of her if the place were not so satisfactory in all other ways. He would talk to the landlady; she would recommend something. The landladies all knew one another in this business.

I complained about his not wanting to look for a place where all three of us could live together, but Tania said he was right. She believed that we were safer without him, and he was safer without us. If the three of us were together, we would be drawing attention to ourselves; all the questions about our situation, why we were living in Warsaw in a rooming house, why we had no other family or friends, would be multiplied and become even harder to answer. The imperative need to avoid attracting attention, even at a cost as great as this, was another leitmotiv of our existence.

Grandfather told us he had not had any problems with the police and only minor problems with blackmailers; nothing expensive. Usually, it was some low-life youth who followed him for a while in the street, then asked for a light and said, Pan looks familiar to me, could he help with a little cash? These people had a look one could not mistake when they made their approach, like pimps in the old days. For the benefit of the landlady, so that she would understand where he got his money, he pretended he dealt in leather coats, the height of fashion in those days, on the black market; that is why he was wearing such a strange garment. His supposed black-market activity meant he had to be out of the apartment several hours each day. Being obliged to find someplace to drag himself to each day probably had kept him from going insane; he was so lonely. There was a *mleczarnia* where he went to eat cheese pierogi and sit over tea. He told Tania that she should not worry about being able to sell a piece of jewelry if she needed to. There was an intelligent jeweler who dealt in everything—stolen goods, Jewish diamonds and gold coins included. The man understood values. When grandfather was short of cash, he paid the jeweler a little visit. He told us he kept a couple of rings taped to his body, just in case it turned out he could not return to the apartment; the rest was hidden under a floorboard he had loosened with a knife. He would show Tania how to do it as soon as we had a place to live. As he talked, the mechanics of existence began to seem less impossible to master. Tania and he agreed that we would meet the next day at the same place, only earlier. He hoped to have addresses of rooms we could look at. When we were about to say good-bye, he started to cry very hard, and as though he had been freed from some restraint that had held him frozen, Tania and I wept with him.

All at once, grandfather wiped his face dry, stood up very straight and said in a loud voice, My dear children, God will bring us consolation, this is His place, let us pray once more for your dear mother's soul. He took Tania and me by the arms and led us up to the side altar. There, he pushed us down to our knees and whispered, Quick, start crossing yourselves, put your hands over your faces and pray. I knew how to do it; Zosia had taught me long ago to make the sign of the cross, and we now crossed ourselves each time we walked by a church. We remained in that position until grandfather whispered that we should cross ourselves again, stand up, and follow him. He showed us at a distance two men who had left the Cathedral and were walking toward the other end of the Rynek. This pair looked to him like real policemen, he said, not the usual trash. He had noticed them standing nearby, studying us with great interest, intently. He was surprised the prayer performance had fooled them; more likely, they didn't want to be seen picking people up in the Cathedral even when it was half-deserted. It was his fault: he should never have allowed us to stay so long on that bench talking. It was bound to attract attention.

By the end of the following week, we were installed at the apartment of Pani Z. in a street off Długa. This lady turned out to be the widow of a physician. Tania discovered the unfortunate coincidence of the late husband's profession over a cup of tea; the deal to rent the room had been concluded. As soon as Tania began to try out her speech about being the wife of a doctor from Lwów and the officers' prison camp in Russia, Pani Z. told Tania about her natural sympathy for the family of a colleague. Tania said she almost spilled her tea when she heard this news, and she continued to think the medical connection meant serious trouble.

There was no doubt about Tania's being able to pass for a doctor's wife. She could display a knowledge of medicine and the honorarium structure of the profession that would do credit to any doctor's wife or widow, as well as an appropriate capacity for instant diagnosis. But what acquaintances might this she-devil of a landlady have among doctors in Lwów, of whom she could inquire, if she felt a stirring of curiosity, about Tania's husband? Would she attempt to look him up in professional lists? Anything like that might be fatal. To begin with, we had no idea of the profession of the man whose name appeared on our papers; that information wasn't required to be mentioned. All we knew was that his name was Tadeusz. That appeared on my birth certificate and Tania's identity card and marriage certificate. But we weren't really sure that such a Tadeusz had ever existed in Lwów or elsewhere. Hertz said the papers were genuine, but he might have been sold very skillful forgeries. It was also possible that he had told Tania they were real only to give her greater self-assurance in the event we were ordered to show them to the police.

The solution was to move, but we couldn't do it immediately; that might arouse suspicion. We would look for another place, rent it, and leave here within two or three weeks, paying Pani Z. a month's rent in place of notice. It was unlikely she would begin prying and get information right away; it was a risk we had to take. Grandfather agreed with this plan. He had not met Pani Z. or come to our room. If he had, his relationship to us would have had to be acknowledged: we three looked alike and it would be hard to lie about it, yet telling Pani Z. that he was Tania's father and my grandfather was awkward, too. Her new maiden name did not match his, and he had not mentioned to his own landlady that he was looking for a room for his daughter and grandson. In fact, he had not told his landlady that his friends had rented a room from Pani Z. That was another precaution; let them talk and put two and two together if they have nothing better to do, but he was not going to make finding us through his landlady easier. He decided that we would see one another every morning, at the Cathedral if it rained, and otherwise in different parts of the Saxon Gardens we would agree on as time passed.

In the meantime, Tania and I were learning the routine of communal apartment living, studying the street map of Warsaw, and rehearsing what she and I should

and should not say at the dining table, Pani Z.'s being
an establishment where eating in one's room was
frowned upon as messy and unfriendly. To make it easier for herself to stay out of Pani Z.'s salon, Tania quietly made it clear that, whenever my health permitted,
she and I would be busy with my lessons in our room.
This was a reason for keeping to ourselves that could
not be criticized or cause undue comment, and yet it
reduced our contacts with Pani Z.

There was a special sort of social occasion, however,
in addition to meals, for which we could not fail to
emerge and join Pani Z. and our fellow lodgers. Since
mid-April, there had been fighting in the Warsaw
ghetto; at the dinner table the lodgers and Pani Z. talked
of little else. Jews had actually attacked Germans, even
forcing the SS unit that was sent to restore order to
retreat. Some said that many of the SS had been killed.
But now Germans were teaching the Jews a final lesson,
and at the end of every afternoon, the weather being
very mild, we all went to the roof under Pani Z.'s direction and gathered around her to watch what she liked
to call our fireworks. She claimed it was the first real
entertainment the Germans had provided in all this sad
time. Pani Z. and her little band were not alone; it
seemed that most of the tenants were on the roof, and
the roofs of adjoining buildings were equally crowded.
No wonder: the view from Długa in the direction of
Zamenhof and the ghetto was almost unobstructed, and
one could hear very well.

People on the roof explained that the Germans were
using artillery. That was why the buildings in the ghetto
were exploding and crumbling. Then they set them on
fire, so that black-and-orange clouds rose in the evening
sky. One could not see it, but in what was left of the
buildings, and in whatever other holes they were hid-

den, Jews were burning. The incineration process was fortunate, our neighbors said: otherwise, decaying corpses would have caused disease that rats could spread far beyond the ghetto. Occasional bets were made on how long it would be until the whole place was one black pile of rubble, and whether any Jews would be left alive inside it.

We did not remain in the house off Długa long enough to see these wagers settled. We left Pani Z.'s according to Tania's plan, moved twice to rooming houses for transients, and, on the day when the SS removed the surviving Jews from the ghetto, we were already living on the other side of the Saxon Gardens, in the apartment of Pani Dumont. We continued to witness the daily spectacle from the roofs of our successive abodes, including Pani Dumont's, until it ended. All of Warsaw was watching with us, but the level of joviality was never again so high. The novelty wore off; also, the view from Pani Z.'s roof had been exceptionally good.

Pani Dumont had met her much regretted late husband, a Walloon railroad engineer, in Kielce, directly after the end of the Great War. He had made his way there as a member of a Belgian relief and technical assistance team. Why Belgians were helping rebuild Polish railroads when their own country had been mauled by the Germans was something Tania wondered about, but that is how Pani Dumont accounted for his presence. She told us that she had learned good French in school and naturally seized the opportunity to practice it with Monsieur Dumont. Her family was hospitable. Romance and marriage followed, they moved to Liège and, after Monsieur Dumont retired, to Warsaw. There his pension went further and enabled them to live comfortably. Monsieur Dumont died in 1940; the Belgian railroad's checks continued to arrive but now bought very little. That was why she had decided to take lodgers. In addition to us, there were living with her the aged, devout widow of a piano teacher; Pan Stasiek, who played the accordion and the harmonica; and the concave-chested, spectacle-wearing Pan Władek. I still sing Pan Stasiek's tunes; almost everything else about him has faded from my memory. Pan Władek became my friend.

Pani Dumont was a large, cheerful woman. All her relatives were still in Kielce; so nothing tied her to Warsaw except the apartment and the income she derived from it. Her lodgers became her substitute family. Monsieur Dumont could not have children; she told Tania that having a young mother with a boy under her roof was a blessing. With Tania's permission, after I became less shy with her, she would teach me French, naturally without cost. Tania was glad to have a kind and apparently well-disposed landlady. On the other hand, the consequence of Pani Dumont's vision of her lodgers was that we were in the same difficulty as at Pani Z.'s. Unless we wanted to distinguish ourselves from the others and possibly antagonize Pani Dumont, we had to spend more time in their company than Tania considered prudent. For instance, the French lessons: Would I be able to learn French from her and not get involved in conversations about Tania and me and about the past that might make me step into a trap? Should Tania ask to be present at the lessons so she could come to the rescue? I assured her that she could count on me; I really wanted to learn French, I would be careful. What about those endless conversations at the dinner table and afterward in Pani Dumont's sitting room? One had to talk, one could not always talk about books, one had to be ready to talk about oneself. Which self? The issue was the limit of one's inventiveness and memory, because the lies had to be consistent—more consistent, according to Tania, than the truth. And they will all be listening, she warned me, don't forget that we are interesting, more interesting than they.

We began to visit my grandfather in his room on Sunday afternoons, in addition to seeing him at the Cathedral, the Saxon Gardens and, later, his *mleczarnia*. He told his landlady Tania was the daughter of his best friend and country neighbor, now dead. There were days I could not go with Tania. I was falling sick again, with long, lingering bouts of bronchitis and, although I saw no children, those few childhood diseases I had not already had. Also, I had my lessons. Pani Dumont took the French lessons very seriously; she found Pani Bronicka to tutor me in general subjects. Unless I was sick, Pani Bronicka came every afternoon except Sunday and left huge assignments to be completed for the next day. She was a *gimnazjum* teacher out of work, the Germans having closed most schools above the primary level. She brought the textbooks we needed. Forming the mind of a nine-year-old who had never been to school appealed to her. She set out to impart to me information and notions of discipline with all the rigor and energy customary in a first-rate state teaching establishment. Giving private lessons was punishable by death, but Pani Bronicka was fearless and needed money. She told me it was a teacher's duty to teach and make it possible for a boy to become an educated man. All she asked was that I keep my part of the bargain, which was to learn.

She approved of the way Tania had taught me to read and discuss what I had read; she undertook to drill me

in compositions: they were to have a beginning, a development and an end. My clumsy slowness in arithmetic appalled her. Above all, she found intolerable my
weak character, by which she meant my habit of insin-
uating flattery. It will not do, she told me, always to be
trying to make oneself liked and then to ask whether
one has succeeded. She wished me to endeavor, quietly
and modestly, to deserve being liked. Our model compositions were on themes from Polish revolutionary his-
tory or, because we were reading Sieńkiewicz, the long
Polish struggle against Ukrainian invaders. Pan Wołodyjowski, the diminutive saber wizard, always hope-
lessly in love, always victorious in a duel, replaced Old
Shatterhand as the hero of my daydreams, at least when
I was not the colonel of my Wehrmacht lead soldier
regiment. At the same time, my lead army was under-
going a degree of reorganization. There was no question that the German soldiers we saw in Warsaw were
winners, but was that the reality? We were listening to
BBC broadcasts with the other lodgers and when we
went to see my grandfather. That was another activity
punishable by death. In Smolensk, on the Dnieper, in
Kiev, the Russians were beating the Germans; perhaps
Stalingrad was not simply a case of von Paulus's incom-
petence or treachery. I began to move some of my better regiments over to the Russian side. Pani Bronicka
intensified our geography lessons. She too listened to
the BBC. She brought a globe to make me understand
that it was not just the Russian front that counted. We
were to have no illusions, the Reich was terribly strong
and dangerous, but one could see thick, heavy arrows
sticking deep in its flanks; the Reich would fall, like a
wild boar.

Meanwhile, I was breaking Pani Bronicka's heart. She
wrote down my assignments in pencil in a little note-

book she had given me. I would erase the page numbers and set myself lighter tasks. After a week or two she caught me: she had recorded the assignment in her own notebook as well. She said it was her duty to tell my mother. I pleaded with her, promising to make up the omitted pages; she relented. I was desperately afraid of Tania. She hated cheating, except to avoid capture; she would sense danger in the effect on Pani Dumont and the other lodgers if my behavior became known. They were all taking an interest in my progress. Pan Władek, who was a chemist, was helping me with arithmetic. But almost immediately after Pani Bronicka forgave me I began to change my assignments again, in exactly the same way. I even cut some pages out of the notebook with a razor blade. This time Tania was informed; my soldiers were confiscated and put in Pani Bronicka's custody until further notice, Tania having somehow propitiated her to the point of agreeing to continue to teach me.

When we were alone, Tania said scornfully that if it was my nature to be a cheat it was too bad that I was not at least original and clever at it. My disgrace was too profound, and Pani Bronicka too visibly upset, for Tania not to tell Pani Dumont. At the evening meal, my case was discussed, the lodgers offering varying assessments of my guilt. Pan Władek's was the worst: he thought that, considering the help I had gotten from him, I was not just lazy, I was evil. He was laughing, rocking back in his chair. I punched him, in his hollow chest, with all my force. The blow threw him against the wall. He coughed; his glasses fell off his nose. It occurred to me that I had done this terrible thing not because of what he had said to me, but because he had put me to shame before Tania. But I was not altogether like Pan Wołodyjowski; I was afraid. I got down on one knee and asked Pan Władek's forgiveness. He said I was not to worry; it was his fault. He had been wrong to tease me when I was unhappy.

The woman at grandfather's apartment, Pani Basia, was definitely Jewish. Right after our first visit, Tania said she must really be Pani Sara. Her son's name was Henryk; he was younger than I, as grandfather had supposed. I thought he was also more stupid, he was not taking lessons from a tutor, and Pani Basia didn't work with him regularly. His collection of lead soldiers was good, better than mine. Before my soldiers were taken away, I brought them with me on my visits. Later, he shared his with me.

We played in my grandfather's room. It seemed to me that grandfather was getting thinner, which made his nose look big and sharp. Ever since Tania had told him about grandmother, he wore a black band on the sleeve of his black coat and only black neckties. Tania worried about how taciturn he had become; she said he talked only when I was there or if she put him on the subject of air raids. He knew the date of every major bombardment of Germany. It was best, he would say, when they came in waves, like the three attacks on Berlin in November and December; that gave them no rest. Although the Germans did not know it, they were becoming hunted animals, like Jews. But the BBC didn't have a raid against Germany to report every day that met my grandfather's standards. The winter wore on sadly, and every Sunday, against grandfather's and Tania's better judgment as to what was prudent behavior, and their promises to each other that we would not go to see him so often, we would be in his room, with a cake or cold meat or fish or whatever else Tania could find that was good and that she knew he liked.

I was playing with Henryk and his soldiers one such Sunday in January 1944 when grandfather and Tania heard something disturbing in the corridor. The door to grandfather's room was always closed. They told Henryk and me to be quiet; we all began to listen carefully. These were men's voices. The landlady was answering them. Then there were footsteps going in the direction of Pani Basia's room, then more voices, and a door being slammed.

Grandfather said, I won't sit here pretending I am deaf, I will speak to the landlady, the three of you stay here and try to be calm. In a moment he returned and told us, You have to be patient. It's the Polish police in civilian clothes; they know about Henryk's mother. But Pani Maria told them she saw Henryk go out with his ice skates; she made sure Pani Basia could hear her. She told them nothing about us. If Pani Basia has any money and any sense, she can buy them off.

We sat in silence, Henryk crying a little. Grandfather got out his cards and made a sign to Tania. They began a game of gin rummy. Grandfather whispered, This is just a pleasant family scene; if they come here, Henryk is our Janek's friend, he came with Janek to visit, you are my oldest friend's daughter, I held you at your baptism, and now stop sniveling and play with your soldiers. A long time passed, and again there were voices and steps in the corridor; Pani Basia was giggling. Grandfather opened the door, looked down the corridor and said, It's all right, the police are gone. We went to Pani Basia's room. The drawers and the wardrobe were open, there were clothes on the floor; they must have searched for money or jewels. She was lying crosswise on the rumpled bed. Her legs were bare; she was very pink in the face. When she saw us, she raised herself and went slowly over to Henryk and then gestured to the table, where there was a bottle of vodka and glasses. They wanted everything, money, liquor, me, she said, and they got all they wanted. They told me they won't be back, they know I have nothing left except more of me and that's not worth much.

I did not see Pani Basia or Henryk again. Tania told grandfather that she could not risk taking me there, that he should move, because they might come back or send their friends. Grandfather refused. He said he would stay right there in his room and might marry his landlady, even though she was older than he and ugly.

Pan Władek asked me why I had the habit of smiling when there was nothing to smile about; it couldn't be because I was stupid, it had to be because I was a little hypocrite. We were at the dinner table, with Pani Dumont and the other lodgers. I didn't know how to answer. Tania answered for me: He does it to be polite. No, said Pan Władek, politeness does not call for pretending about one's feelings except to avoid hurting another person. Our Janek is a hypocrite. And then he asked whether I knew if hypocrisy was a venial or a mortal sin. This time the piano teacher's widow intervened. The question was too difficult. How could I know when I had not even been to catechism class; Pan Władek was wrong to try to confuse me. Until I received instruction, it was enough for me to remember never to lie. But, she continued, turning to Tania, Isn't it time for dear Janek to prepare himself for his first Communion? Father P. will be leading a class himself, Janek could be ready by May. With Pani Tania's permission she would be happy to introduce me to the priest.

There was approval of this new step in my education all around the table. Only Pan Władek mumbled something about how priests made hypocrites and pharisees and how that was not what he had intended when he undertook to draw me into a frank conversation. When we got up from the table, he surprised and frightened me again: Would Pani mind, he asked Tania, if Janek talked to me for a few minutes, alone?

I had never been in Pan Władek's room before. It was furnished like ours, except for a large armchair in which Pan Władek sat down after lighting his acetylene lamp. He asked me to sit in the straight chair at the table and told me he was very sorry about what had happened; this time I must forgive him. Sometimes watching my mother and me struggle so hard became unbearable; he wanted me to be, if only for a moment, like other boys. Anyway, we were doing too much. Nobody needed to be so perfect. I was to go to my room now and tell my mother not to worry. He was our friend.

Tania was furious. She said he could only mean that he had guessed the truth, and if that was the case, his conduct was inexcusable. He was drawing attention to me, he had put us in a position about the first Communion she had wanted to avoid. She hoped, but wasn't sure, that this was not his way of confirming his suspicions before he blackmailed or denounced us. She would talk to grandfather about it.

My grandfather listened carefully. We were in the *mleczarnia* eating cheese *naleśniki*. He thought that this Władek of ours would not have waited so long if he had bad intentions, but that he might be indiscreet. Probably I should avoid conversations with him. If he was a good man, he would understand and would not hold it against us. Helping a Jew to hide was an action that Poles were shot for; Pan Władek ought to prefer not knowing about us and above all ought to prefer not letting anyone else think that he knew. It was lucky the Russians would be with us soon. Kiev was not so far away; before long, the Wehrmacht would begin to crumble. We were all too tired to keep up the pretense if they made us wait. Just this morning a man had stopped him in the street and asked to see his papers: the usual face, the usual clothes, the usual voice. If Pan doesn't want trouble, perhaps we can settle it right away, conveniently, at this gate—they went into the gateway of a building on Miodowa, near the theater. The man looked at the papers and said, If Pan lets down his trousers here, it will save us the trouble of going to the police station, Pan knows that once we are there that's the end for him. Grandfather was ready. While the man was busy with the papers, he had opened his jackknife inside his coat pocket. Now he took it out and said, Here is my penis if you want to check it, and take yours out, so I can cut it off. They parted, grandfather said, on the best of terms, but he wasn't sure he had the strength to deal with more of these robbers.

We went to see Father P. without the widow. Tania worried about having her at the interview; she thought it would make us both more nervous. The priest studied my birth certificate, returned it to Tania, and said that unquestionably it was time to begin my religious instruction. He regretted that my health did not allow me to attend school; so far, the authorities had not prevented pastoral work in the classroom, and Pani could well understand that the nation's spiritual capital could not be preserved without letting children come to the Lord as early as possible. The class would start next Monday; it would meet in the afternoon. He wished me success. As we were leaving, he said that he knew about us; the widow had spoken to him about Tania's charm and high cultural level and about my young intelligence. He was surprised that he had not met Tania sooner and had not seen us in the congregation. Tania said she felt remiss. We did come here to Mass, but not every Sunday. She was trying to acquaint me with church architecture. That is why, if the weather and my health permitted, we made pilgrimages to churches in different parts of the city presenting particular points of interest; I was already familiar with Father P.'s beautiful church. As for her, she had gone to confession in the Cathedral when we first came to Warsaw and wanted to continue to seek spiritual direction there.

The catechism class was held in a room behind the sacristy that was cold and smelled of sweat. Tania would come with me, stay in the church until the lesson was over, and then quickly lead me away. She didn't want me to wait for her after class, she didn't want me to get into conversations with the other children, and she didn't want me to walk home alone. I knew that was what she would decide, and although I did not tell her, I was glad. I had become afraid of other boys. Also, now that food was very expensive and hard to find, my appetite had become voracious. I dreamed about eating and ate too much whenever I could. I had become fat, with a round little stomach. Polish children were usually thin; I had always been thin in the past. I thought the boys in the catechism class would pick on me because of my fat stomach.

Father P. gave us a book of questions and answers and prayers to study. He led us in prayer; Tania told me to watch carefully how the other boys prayed, when they knelt down, when they crossed themselves, and to do the same. It was all right to be a little slow, but I should not let it be noticed that I didn't know the custom. Then Father P. spoke about the subject for the day and called on us by name to answer the questions in the book. He read them aloud slowly. I found it was best to give the answers exactly as written in the book. I also found, as I studied the book and listened to Father P., that my personal situation was desperate and despicable.

There was no salvation except through grace, and grace could be acquired only through baptism. It was true that Jesus took with Him to heaven, when He ascended, the virtuous ancients who died before He came, but that door to salvation was now closed. I asked Father P. whether savages living in our time away from the church could be saved if they were good, and he was very clear about it: the ministry of Jesus was complete. Virtue without grace could not suffice. He explained it by the example of the Jewish people. The patriarchs of the Old Testament were included in the harrowing of hell. But after the Lord's birth, the Jews broke their covenant with God, crucified His Son, and remained rebellious to His teaching. It was evident that every Jew, even if he did not break the Commandments, was damned.

If that was true, my case was worse than that of a savage. A savage might live in ignorance of Jesus, but I was born and lived in a Catholic nation; it was my father's and now my own decision to reject life in

Christ. And it could not even be said that I was not breaking the Ten Commandments. Bearing false witness was forbidden; serious lying and hypocrisy were the same as bearing false witness; I was a liar and a hypocrite every day; I was mired in mortal sin on that account alone, even if all the other evil in me was disregarded. It was, of course, possible for me to be baptized. I now knew that this was a sacrament that could not ordinarily be repeated, so that it would be necessary to find a priest to whom we could reveal that I was a Jew and had not been baptized before. Baptism would wash away the Original Sin I was born with and, I thought, my other accumulated sins as well, but how could I go on lying and not fall again into mortal sin that would put me on the road to damnation? On the other hand, even if Father P. was wrong about virtuous persons who had not received baptism being damned—and that was Tania's opinion—even if my lying could be forgiven without confession, true repentance and absolution, was I good? I was impure in my thoughts, that was a mortal sin, and I was going to commit blasphemy, the gravest sin of all, when I took Communion without baptism and after a false confession.

I argued these questions in my head and with Tania, without mentioning to her sins other than the ones she knew about, and begged her to find a pretext for me not to profane the host. Her answer never varied: You have to do it, it's not your fault, if Jesus Christ allows these things to happen it is the fault of Jesus Christ, not your fault. She forbade me to speak to grandfather about this nonsense.

Meanwhile, the god of war seemed to be deserting the Reich. Russian troops were in the Bukovina, they reached the Czechoslovakian border; in a space of two days they took Odessa and Kerch. Pani Bronicka's and my grandfather's excitement was intense. I wished they could meet, but that was judged to be out of the question. On the map we studied, Pani Bronicka drew lines that showed the directions Russian armies were taking: in the north, where they were thrusting into Lithuania, commanded generals whose names were unknown to us; Zhukov's and Rokossovsky's troops were like daggers aimed at the heart of Poland. Only they were not going to stab us: German blood would flow, was already flowing. Pan Władek and Pan Stasiek had been at the Central Station. Many of their friends had also gone. Train after train of wounded German soldiers headed west. The men were terrifying to see: dirty, with bandaged heads and crazy eyes. In Warsaw, there were attacks by the underground on SS men; in the countryside, trains were derailed and attacked. The SS was taking hostages. Pawiak prison was said to be full of them. Sporadically, they would be shot in the street by Wehrmacht firing squads. Before the execution, the Germans would fill their mouths with cement. That was to stop them from crying out or singing the national anthem.

Everything edible was rationed. Black-market prices rose to levels that made Tania stingy. Grandfather was also nervous about money. One day, Tania came from the market with pork she had gotten at a decent price, probably because it was an inferior cut. She cooked it especially long; she was worried about trichinosis. When we sat down to supper that night, we alone had meat before us. Tania said we would share, and served portions for everybody. The meat had an odd taste; it was sweet. Pan Władek said he would show it to a veterinarian; perhaps Tania had been sold horse meat. He took a piece with a bone. Next day he told her in secret there was no doubt we had eaten man.

Grandfather's jeweler disappeared. We had to have cash. Both Tania and grandfather thought it was dangerous not to have a reasonable supply of bank notes on hand. If a man in the street had to be paid off, one could not hand him a ring. He would never again leave one alone. Tania said she knew a person who might help, Pani Wodolska, the widow of a professor of philosophy at the university in Cracow. Her husband had been fond of Tania, she had often been a guest at their house; the widow was in Warsaw, she would find her. Grandfather remembered the name only vaguely; he did not object. Somehow, Tania got the address and went to see Pani Wodolska alone and unannounced. She returned perplexed. Pani Wodolska recognized her immediately, was very cordial, and said she knew jewelers who might help. She might even know someone for gold coins. Wouldn't it be best if Pani Tania brought all her things to her house the next day? They could look them over together and decide what should be sold and what should be kept. Tania said that might be difficult. Our things were split up, in the custody of different friends; it was necessary to be very discreet about going to their houses; she would see what she could do and certainly bring the one or two pieces she had at hand. Grandfather said, Don't go back there. They quarreled about it. Tania thought cash was worth taking a risk for. Pani Wodolska was a prewar lady. How could she understand the dangers we were running or how little trust we had? She would show her two rings and a chain.

That is what she did. They agreed on the lowest acceptable price; Pani Wodolska asked Tania to stop by in two days, in the afternoon. She was sure that the affair would be concluded by then. Tania kept the appointment, leaving me at home. She returned very late, so late that I had become frightened. She said she was tired; she would say what had happened only if I promised not to repeat it to grandfather. Then she told me that, when she arrived, Pani Wodolska had asked her what other pieces she had brought. Tania was startled and told her none, she thought that was all we were selling. What you gave me were false stones set in gold-plated tin, replied Pani Wodolska. That is an old Jewish peddler trick, and I have the police waiting for you.

There was, in fact, a man in the apartment, who came in and sat down on a chair near the wall when Pani Wodolska rang. They finally allowed Tania to leave in exchange for the bracelet and the ring she was wearing and the contents of her wallet. It took her so long to return because she went about in circles, trying to make sure she was not being followed.

The day of my first Communion came. Tania offered to give me breakfast on the sly in our room, but I refused. I wanted to be clean inside, just as Father P. had directed. The entire household, except for Pan Władek, who was not feeling well, went to church with Tania and me. Father P. had heard my confession the day before. I had gone over my sins with Tania to be sure there were just enough and that I did not try to be too clever. The priest blessed me. He told me to say the Creed twice, the Our Father five times and the Hail Mary as many times as I could and still pay attention. I did it all carefully and slowly, and even though I knew I remained in the state of mortal sin, I tried to do nothing, until I knelt to receive the wafer, that would add to the weight of the judgment hanging over me.

Dante's *disdain: his disdain for the damned. They are naked, the reader knows it, yet Dante never misses an opportunity to point to that degrading circumstance. Take the tongue-lashing he administers, albeit with a touch of sanctimonious hesitation due to the subject's exalted rank, to Pope Nicholas III, who sold church offices. Virgil approves of this boorish harangue. A satisfied look comes over his face as he listens to his disciple. In general, Virgil likes Dante's disdainful soul, alma sdegnosa.*

Dante's damned also can be disdainful or, at least, unbowed. Brunetto Latini, sprinting along the burning sand with a band of sodomites, lifting his feet with the greatest possible speed from the fire, is like one running the race for the green flag in Verona, and seems to be among those who win and not those who lose—Dante uses the respectful voi *when he speaks to him. Heretic Farinata rises upright in the tomb where he is baking to address Dante, as though he held hell in great disdain,* com'avesse l'inferno in gran dispitto. *Under flakes of fire falling slowly, like snow in the mountains when there is no wind, lies Capaneus, disdainful and scowling,* dispettoso e torto; *his pride is unquenched. And Vanni Fucci, tormented by serpents, makes the sign of the fig with both hands, crying, Take them, God, I am aiming at you,* Togli, Dio, ch'a te le squadro! *Ostensibly, these are instances of punishment that for mysterious reasons is not working: fire does not mature Capaneus, the bestial Vanni Fucci is unripe,* acerbo, *and the reader is not apt to take him into his heart. But what reader, even of those who have sane intellects,* li'ntelletti sani, *does*

*not, in his heart of hearts, admire Brunetto and Fari-
nata, even the blaspheming giant Capaneus, precisely
for their disdain?*

*Why is this so? The grandfather's and Tania's brav-
ery and occasional defiance were admirable, but then
the punishment the Germans piled on them in the hell
of Poland was undeserved, and they were morally right
to defy it. In the* Inferno, *the punishment is always deserved, a primordial part of the universal order over
which presides the God of Love. And yet, when proud
or physically courageous damned are defiant and disdainful, admiration and even pity stir in the heart. Why
is this so in the* Commedia *and in life? We should more
properly be outraged at these sinners' failure to welcome their torments meekly, assuming as we must, that
their crimes are abhorrent and that Minòs, that con-
noisseur of sins,* conoscitor de le peccata, *has consigned
them to fit punishments. Why does a Jew, hunted by the
Gestapo, captured, and on his way to the gas chamber,
have to be disdainful or defiant to awaken sympathy,
avoid disdain? Why cluck one's tongue over the courage
of fat Göring at Nuremberg? In the vestibule of hell
dwell the sorry souls of those who lived without infamy
and without praise. These wretches run in a long train
after a banner, naked, as Dante takes the trouble to
emphasize, and stung by gadflies and wasps so that
blood mixed with tears streaks their faces. It is clear
that Dante disdains them more than any of the other
damned: neither heaven nor deep hell will receive them;
mercy and justice scorn them; Virgil refuses to discuss
their condition. Why are they worse than the damned
who lived in infamy and were notorious on this earth
for their sins? Why do we find it so difficult to admire
those who are tormented and make no defiant gesture?*

Suppose they are neither meek nor proud, only frightened. Why do we care whether a fallen demon outshines legions thought bright?

V

SHORTLY AFTER MY FIRST COMMUNION, I TURNED YEL-
low. My liver hurt and I was feverish. It was obvious
to Tania that I had jaundice, like my grandmother just
before the end. Through my previous maladies Tania
had treated me with aspirin, compresses and chicken
bouillon. Summoning a doctor was excluded; he would
want to examine me, he might see my penis. I was not
a girl, and we were not in old China: I could not show
the physician what hurt me by pointing, from behind a
curtain, to the body of an ivory doll. This time, Tania
was worried. She was not sure how my father cured
jaundice. Apparently, Pan Władek was worried too. He
came to our room and said, I can recommend a doctor
you can trust in every way; please let him examine the
child, Pani need not be afraid. Tania agreed. The diet
and pills the doctor prescribed worked rapidly. I was
able to resume lessons and even to go out to meet my
grandfather.

It was a glorious hot summer, one sun-filled day suc-
ceeding another. As my grandfather had foreseen, the
Wehrmacht was crumbling in the East. In three weeks,
fifteen German divisions were annihilated; in the two
or three weeks that followed, the Russians advanced
almost four hundred kilometers. We had already seen
an army routed and in full retreat: the Red Army fleeing
from T. in June 1941. But at that time, from the outset,

the front was never far from us, and then the Russians seemed to disappear overnight. Now we saw a defeat as though in slow motion: trucks in the streets of Warsaw as well as trains with German wounded, trucks and trains with bedraggled units being withdrawn from the front—all heading west. One heard of German soldiers asking to be hidden or to trade their pistols and rifles for civilian clothes.

Meanwhile, the police were everywhere. Feldgendarmerie patrols were stationed at important intersections. There were more and more controls of identification papers and random arrests. A loudspeaker would suddenly bellow over a marketplace with orders to freeze, and police, sometimes only Germans and sometimes Germans and Poles, would appear from abutting streets and search the crowd. On certain days, Pan Władek advised us not to go out; it seemed that he no longer went to work; he would leave the apartment and reappear at unusual hours. On other days he would ask Tania and sometimes me to carry packages for him. We were to hand them over to such and such person who would approach us at a specified place. He said it was as safe as anything else we did.

Then, toward the end of July, the Russians astonishingly slowed down. We could not understand how they could have been stopped. The BBC told us, in its usual brisk and cheerful manner, that they were regrouping and shortening their supply lines. Fresh troops from the Dnieper were advancing to the front. But fresh German troops were also being brought on the line. There was talk in Warsaw of long German convoys, this time heading east. The RAF and, as some thought, the Russians bombarded Warsaw during several nights. Tania told me to welcome the thud of the bombs and the whine of a diving plane that almost always preceded them. We were learning to guess, according to the depth and rich-ness of the thud, whether a building had been hit. Sometimes the thud was very loud and very near and the walls and ceiling of the cellar, where our whole building took shelter, would suddenly sway. A raid sel-dom lasted long. We would go back upstairs and get into bed, our hearts filled with hope. These planes were a friendly presence; they could not stay but they would return.

Pan Władek and Pan Stasiek now openly referred to Armia Krajowa, or A.K., which stood for Home Army, the main branch of the Polish resistance directed by the government in London. They brought leaflets that had appeared in the streets calling on the population to rise and rally to the Polish colors. A.K. was ready to strike at the enemy and liberate Warsaw. According to Pan Władek, they were only waiting for the Russians to com-plete their preparations and resume the offensive. But the Russians did not seem to be moving at all. The positions reported by the BBC were unchanged; for the time being, the front in Poland was stationary.

The only trace left of my jaundice was an excessively refined sense of smell; I could tell what meal was being cooked in each apartment in the building. Unfortu-nately, just then meals were especially malodorous. Sometimes I would reel from nausea. Tania took me to the Saxon Gardens to breathe fresh air. We went on ever longer walks.

August 1 was a Tuesday. We met my grandfather in his *mleczarnia*. Almost no food to be had anymore. We had some bread and tea. Grandfather said he felt an uncomfortable sort of quiet in the city. At the same time, there had been more leaflets about liberating Warsaw. He didn't like it. He thought Tania should carefully stock some provisions, never mind how much things cost. She should buy candles if she couldn't get acetylene, flour, rice, bacon, whatever she could find. We decided to meet again the next day. He told us to take the trolley home and buy the provisions. He took a trolley himself and went back to Mokotów.

In fact, we did not take the trolley. A sort of laziness overcame us. We went first to the Saxon Gardens and sat in the sun. We were wondering whether my father was alive. Neither of us could imagine when the end of the war would come or where we would be at that time or where he might look for us if he reappeared from Russia. I thought it would be best to wait for him in T. We would get our house back, perhaps find our furniture, and begin to live as before. He certainly would have the same idea; he would go to T. We headed in the direction of the Cathedral and the Rynek Starego Miasta, the Old Town market. The streets were full of people strolling about; one felt a mood of gaiety out of keeping with the Wehrmacht and Feldgendarmerie squads in battle dress on Teatralny and Zamkowy. They had armored cars; the machine guns on street corners were surrounded by sandbags. We ate a roll in the Rynek, watching the crowd. It felt strangely difficult to return to Pani Dumont's: Tania said for the moment we were free, the house was like a prison cell. But we had to go back. Though we were tired, Tania thought we should take advantage of the late afternoon sun and walk. It was time to start.

We were still in the narrow, gray streets of the Old Town when we began to hear, seemingly from all sides, the sound of rapid gunfire, then the sound of machine guns, and then much louder sounds, which we would later recognize as the explosion of hand grenades. People ran in the street; other people shouted for everyone to get off the street, into entranceways of buildings or wherever else one could find cover. We ducked into an entrance gate, like many such gates in Warsaw really a porte-cochère leading from the street into the inner yard, which someone immediately began to try to shut; it was stuck and left us a view of the street. Clattering down Piwna in the direction of the Rynek was a Wehrmacht armored car, the barrel of its machine gun moving carefully from side to side, firing in regular, short bursts. We could see the tracers, then the holes that the bullets made in the buildings, and the shattering of glass. From up high, a window or a roof, someone began to shoot at the armored car, and bullets were ricocheting from its sides. The car stopped, raised its machine gun, and returned fire. This lasted awhile, until a cylindrical object, like a small glass bottle, rolled toward the rear of the armored car and under it. For a moment nothing seemed to happen. Then there came a loud explosion, smoke, and the car began to burn. German soldiers got out; other men could be seen kneeling on the sidewalk and taking aim. The soldiers fell. Everybody in the porte-cochère was talking at once: we began to understand what was happening. Before our very eyes, probably throughout Warsaw, the A.K. was attacking the Germans. The uprising that Pan Władek thought was to await a new Russian offensive had begun; that could only mean that the Russians were coming. Tomorrow or perhaps within a few days at the latest, we would be free; we would never have to hide or be afraid again.

Instead, weeks passed and the fighting in the city continued. Until the Germans cut the electricity, we listened to the news. According to the BBC, the Russians were still consolidating their positions and shortening supply lines. The Wehrmacht radio told us that

German reinforcements had been brought to the periphery of Warsaw. The BBC knew that but hoped that the Red Army would liberate the city before long; pending that event, airdrops of weapons and ammunition would sustain its heroic defenders. The Wehrmacht radio promised the population of Warsaw prompt extermination. We were beginning to joke that perhaps the Americans would get to us sooner than the Russians.

Meanwhile, the Luftwaffe, flying very low, was bombing and burning Warsaw in a wheel of fire; we, in the Old Town, were the hub of that wheel. Progressively, the wheel became smaller. Until the bombs began to fall regularly quite near us, we went up on the roof to watch the planes, the bombs they dropped, and the fires. In appearance these new German fireworks were not unlike those in the flaming ghetto we had earlier observed from Pani Z.'s. Only this time, we and our fellow watchers were a part of the spectacle, and no one on the roof was cheering. The university library was hit and burned; for days afterward, in addition to the steady rain of undifferentiated ash to which we were now accustomed, entire calcined pages of books fell from the sky. Sometimes they were stuck together and did not break up when they hit the ground; one could make out large portions of the text.

We had been in the house on Piwna for perhaps a week when a woman lawyer who had also found herself there because she was visiting her corset maker's workshop on the third floor of the building began to smile and wink at Tania and then to talk to her. It was the evening; as usual we were in the cellar. Tania asked her to sit down with us on the mattress she had bought from the janitor's wife, Pani Danuta; Tania still seethed from the unpleasantness of the transaction. To my surprise, she began to tell this stranger how, for days after she had paid the extortionate price, the janitress came to the cellar, looked the mattress over, and speaking to no one in particular explained that Tania had driven a hard bargain, acquired the precious object for half its value and was lucky to have made the deal before other homeless, more willing to open their wallets, got hold of every spare mattress and cot in the building. Pani Danuta was tired of all the homeless—begging, whining and needing everything just because they had nothing. They should have stayed in their own apartments, with their own furniture, food and clothes instead of trying to live off the kindness of poor people who would soon be hungry and naked themselves.

The lawyer laughed and asked that Tania call her by her first name; she used a diminutive, Pani Helenka. Let Pani put herself in the janitress's place, she said. Now these people have three armies to hate: the Wehrmacht, because it is German; Armia Krajowa, because it started this accursed uprising; and the invading army of the homeless, yourself, your son and me and all the others who have been thrust into their midst by bad luck—happening to be on Piwna at the wrong hour of the wrong afternoon. And we all want their mattresses and their food! Pani Danuta and many of the others here see that there is something wrong with this uprising—while the Russians were winning and the Germans were running away our A.K. warriors passed out pamphlets and perhaps shot a German here and a collaborator there. Then just as the Wehrmacht managed to stop the Russians, the boys began their war! Is that the coordination with the Russians and the English they were promising? If they planned to have all of Warsaw destroyed, like Stalingrad, they could not be doing a better job. In any case, the woman means no real harm;

Pani isn't from Warsaw and can't know this class of people. Among them a sharp tongue is often the sign of a soft heart.

Pani Helenka had short, curly gray hair, a round face with round brown eyes, and a round little body. Her gray silk sleeveless blouse was stretched tight over a large bust thrust forward and fortified by a corset I could glimpse under her arms when she gesticulated. She liked to talk; as she warmed up to her subject, she stroked Tania's hair. It was the first time I had seen a stranger be so familiar with Tania. It did not surprise me that Tania submitted; we were in no position to offend Pani Helenka. But it was also the first time since we left Lwów that I heard Tania express her real feelings about anyone except to my grandfather and me.

The cellar was dank; the walls, floor and wooden support beams were all wet to the touch. Pani Helenka bought a salmon pink quilt on credit from her corset maker. All three of us could huddle under it at night, sleeping fitfully, Tania whispering that I must not be afraid when we heard bombs and gunfire approach. During the day, Pani Helenka presided over a bridge game with Tania and a childless couple who moved their mattress so that it faced ours. I watched their hands. When they weren't bidding, we listened to Pani Helenka. Her own apartment, where she also received clients, was in Mokotów, not far from my grandfather's. She had a telephone, but there was nobody to answer it so it was quite useless: we couldn't get a message through to him even if the line weren't down. She had let her secretary go a long time ago. There are no more clients, she laughed, just the black market. She blamed the A.K. not only for having started the uprising when it was unprepared and outnumbered, but especially for having attacked in the afternoon of a working day, so that Warsaw's working people were away from their homes—unless, of course, like her corset maker they worked where they lived. Don't think just of people like yourself and your boy, you were out enjoying the good weather—thank God you are together—or an old maid like me with nobody to care about who decided to have a fitting for some oversized bras, she said addressing Tania. Think of all the mothers who were at work and left their children unattended, children who were sent to play with friends in some park, old people left behind locked doors of their room while whatever niece takes care of them went to work or to shop, all of them lost in a city that has become a bombing-practice target for the Luftwaffe. These are the tragedies that break my heart; people won't let the A.K. forget them.

The Germans cut off the water as well. Going to the toilet was a harrowing problem; the building we were in had no outhouses. With a pickax, the janitor and some other men managed to lift enough paving stones in the yard to allow them to dig a hole. They covered it with boards, leaving a narrow space so that one could empty a chamber pot or even use it directly. Before, we and the other homeless had to ask someone's kind permission to respond to a call of nature or to wash our body or clothes. Now we were at least on a footing of equality. Somebody said, It serves the tenants of this building right; let them start growing petunias in their toilets.

It became harder and harder to get food. Householders sitting in their apartments ate whatever they had gotten ready from well-developed wartime habit or because like my grandfather they sensed that the storm was about to break: potatoes, rice, dried beans and flour. We had to talk them into selling some of these provisions. Tania let Pani Helenka conduct the negotiations on our behalf, but soon no one was foolish enough to exchange necessities for paper that was probably worthless. It became a matter of begging. An A.K. officer tried to instill a spirit of sharing in the building, but no such spirit developed. As the days wore on, the elation of August 1 was turning into resentment and sometimes outright fury against the underground, just as Pani Helenka had foreseen.

Tania's worry about my grandfather was extreme. He was alone, and as a Jew he continued to be in special danger. We also realized how right he had been: we should not have dawdled in the Old Town. We kept daydreaming aloud about somehow finding our way to him, but there was no reasonable prospect of it. His room in Mokotów was practically at the other end of Warsaw, so far that Pani Helenka said she would stop us by force if we tried to go there. In fact, although we did not know it yet, just crossing the street in the Old Town could be a deadly business. Soon, our daydreams had to take another direction. An A.K. man told Tania that the Germans were already in control of Mokotów. We now had to hope that grandfather had not been killed in the fighting. In that case, if we also survived, we would be reunited after the war.

Pani Dumont's apartment was less remote than Mokotów. Tania decided we should try to return there: the jewelry was in its hiding place under a floorboard; we would have clothes and, unless the others had helped themselves to it, Tania's small stock of provisions. We would be surrounded by familiar faces: Tania said that she had never before imagined missing Pani Dumont— Pani Helenka's attentiveness was becoming oppressive. Thus, early one morning, after a brief embrace to bid Pani Helenka farewell, we started out. Tania thought we could manage a few blocks at a time before we were forced to seek temporary shelter. I would go first, running along the sidewalk, keeping low and trying not to make noise. Every couple of houses, I was to stop in an entrance gate and wait for Tania. It was better that I go first because the Germans might not bother about a child; if we went together, we would make a larger and more attractive target. Tania promised she would not be far behind.

The street was empty except for us; I felt very nimble and swift. The gates to buildings were closed, but, even so, in every porte-cochère there was just enough space to squeeze into between the sidewalk and the closed gate itself for me to have a protected corner to crouch in. When Tania reached the gate where I had paused, she would kneel beside me, tell me which new gate to head for and when to start. But at the corner we had to cross Piwna; just turning the corner made no sense.

I could see an entranceway with a closed gate and a good hiding place diagonally across the street. Tania said to run as fast as I could, never mind keeping low this time. I had barely reached the entrance and settled myself against the wall, though, when I heard gunfire, and bullets began scraping the ornamental stone post on my side of the gate and the sidewalk in front of me. A German soldier on the roof of a building on the side of Piwna I had just left, a few doors away from the corner, was shooting at me. So long as I had stayed on his side of the street he had not seen me and I had not seen him. Now each of us had a good view of the other. He was kneeling next to a chimney; from time to time he looked at me through his field glasses. After a while, he stopped firing if I remained very still. As soon as I moved, a single bullet and sometimes two would zing past me. I realized that while he was there Tania could not cross Piwna and come to my gate. He would kill her in the middle of the street.

I didn't have a watch, but I thought hours must have gone by while I stayed at the gate. Occasionally Tania waved to me; she was making signs with her hands that I couldn't understand. Then she disappeared inside her gate. Once in a while, on my side of the street, a door would creak open, and the German would immediately send a bullet or two in its direction. Sometimes it was the same system as with me: silence and then shots. I thought that these were buildings where people were also hiding in entranceways or trying to come out. Once he must have hit somebody, because there was a cry followed for a long time by moaning.

Two more Germans appeared on the roof carrying a machine gun; they set it up and startèd firing along my side of the street, spraying the entranceways carefully, as though with a water hose. The noise was deafening. I had become less frightened when I saw that the first German could not get me; now I was terrified again. More gunfire came from another direction. The Germans continued firing, but no longer at the street. Something was going on from one roof to another; the shooting became continuous. I decided I would try to open the gate and sneak inside while the Germans were busy with other targets, but they were watching me too: when I began to move bullets hit my gate and the post behind which I was hiding.

Abruptly, help came. The gate behind me swung open, someone was firing from behind it in the direction of the Germans, someone else pulled me inside, the gate shut. Inside were Tania and two A.K. soldiers. The men had led her through a sewer below the street to an adjacent building and then through a passage be-

tween the courtyards to my gate. They said we must
hurry, and we followed them to a crowded cellar. The
arrival of the A.K. men caused a stir. One of them
asked everybody to be quiet; he introduced us as having
been trapped in the street by German fire and asked
that we be made welcome.

The new cellar was quite light, for it had half-moon
windows near the ceiling, opening on the street and
courtyard, that had not been boarded up. People were
sitting on beds and chairs; there was a great deal of
conversation. Some of the women spoke to Tania. I
heard her say she was sorry we would be a burden for
them. But these seemed to be strangely generous people: right away, someone offered us biscuits and jam;
another person was looking for a mattress and quilt we
could use; there was a family willing to have us sleep
in their apartment when it was safe to be upstairs.

We remained in this second cellar until the last days
of August. By then, Warsaw lay in ruins, with only a
few buildings in the center of the city intact above the
second floor. All talk of an A.K. victory had ceased.
One could hope that Rokossovsky's army, immobile on
the other side of the Vistula, would finally storm Warsaw and drive the Germans out. But were we more likely
to survive a German or a Russian attack? The odds
seemed even save in one respect: we heard rumors that
in neighborhoods where the Germans had succeeded in
stamping out A.K. resistance they either killed the ci-
vilians on the spot or took them away to camps.

In the meantime, we went about our daily chores. At
night, we took turns going through jagged passages the
A.K. had chopped in walls to a courtyard at the end of
the block where there was a well and a pump. The
training I had received from Pan Kramer in T. became
useful again; I could show Warsaw grown-ups at what

rhythm to pump, and how a bucket that was only three-fourths full was easier to carry and would not spill. Once again, there was very little to eat. Someone from another building—the general opinion was that none of us could have been guilty of such ignominy—broke into the kitchens of several apartments and looted them. The loss of provisions was considerable. Guards were posted. The building decided that the remaining food would be pooled and rationed by a committee of cooks. Several of the older people were sick. Tania volunteered to be a nurse, dispensing aspirin, which was very scarce, applying compresses and cups. A.K. soldiers became a regular presence in the cellar; they needed to sleep for a few hours, some were wounded. The fighting in the streets was drawing closer. We were constantly being bombed and strafed by the Luftwaffe. The A.K. had no antiaircraft guns; they tried to shoot at the planes from the roofs with rifles. Machine guns were scarce and ammunition for them was running out. Once, before it became too dangerous to go to the roof, we watched them hit a plane that had been flying low, from time to time dropping a bomb. It began to smoke and then burn and finally disappeared among distant buildings. Perhaps it returned to the airfield. Now there was no going to the roof or resting in an apartment during pauses in the bombardment. We waited for the end in the cellar.

One afternoon, an A.K. officer came to speak to the people in the cellar. He said that the A.K. would have to withdraw at once from the neighborhood through the sewers; the Germans could be expected within a few hours. We should stay calm and, when the Germans did come, follow their orders promptly and without argument. They would make us leave the building; it was a good idea to gather whatever clothes we needed and have a little suitcase ready. The Germans had Ukrainian guards with them. The Ukrainians were like wild animals. It would be best if young women put shawls over their heads and faces and tried to be inconspicuous. He saluted and wished us all luck. Soon afterward, a bomb fell on the building next to us; another made a hole in the street. People from the building that had been hit came to our cellar. There was less gunfire, and after a while both the gunfire and the bombs began to seem more distant. It was already dark, and the Germans had not come. Few people slept that night. Families sat together talking. Some people prayed aloud.

Tania told me to lie down on our mattress. She lay down too, put her arms around me and talked to me in a whisper. She said it was lucky that we had not forgotten for a moment we were Catholic Poles and that nobody seemed to suspect us. Our only hope was to be like all the others. The Germans weren't going to kill every Pole in Warsaw; there were too many of them, but they would kill every Jew they could catch. We would make ourselves very small and inconspicuous, and we would be very careful not to get separated in the crowd. If something very bad happened and she was taken away, I wasn't to try to follow: it wouldn't help her and I might even make things worse for both of us. If possible I should wait for her. Otherwise, I should take the hand of whatever grown-up near me had the nicest face, say I was an orphan, and hope for the best. I shouldn't say I was a Jew, or let myself be seen undressed if I could avoid it. She had me repeat these instructions and told me to go to sleep.

We were awake when they arrived late the next morning. It was the same bellowing as for Jews in T., the same pounding of rifle butts on the gate and then on the cellar door and the apartment doors and people trying to hurry and stumbling on the stairs. A Wehrmacht officer and a couple of German soldiers stood on the sidewalk in a little group apart while the work was done by Ukrainians: they rushed around, pushing and hitting people as they came out into the street. Some of them had whips and some had dogs. A woman just ahead of us did not move fast enough to satisfy a Ukrainian. He hit her with his whip. Her husband pushed his way in front of her. Two Ukrainians beat him. Many people from other buildings were already assembled in a column, four abreast, ready to march. A Ukrainian called for silence and asked that all the women in our group immediately give up their jewelry. He pointed to a bucket. Then he told us to pass by it one by one. When our turn came, Tania took off her bracelet and ring and threw them in. He asked to see her hands and waved us ahead. I looked at Tania. She had put a kerchief over her head and tied it under her chin; her face was smeared black with coal dust; she was walking bent over like an old woman. When we reached the column she said she wanted to be in the middle of a row; I could be on the outside. The column seemed ready to march when another squabble erupted: a woman had not thrown anything into the bucket; the Ukrainian in charge of it grabbed her hand, saw a ring, beat her on the face and with an easy, fluid gesture, just like a butcher, cut off her finger. He held it up for all to see. There was a ring on it. The finger and ring both went into the bucket.

The march began. Tania had maneuvered us both into the middle of the row, with a man on either side. We no longer saw familiar faces. People from our building had drifted away; much rearranging had to be done before the German officer gave the order for departure. The column went down Krakowskie Przedmieście, turned right on Aleje Jerozolimskie, but it was difficult to recognize in the smoldering ruins the streets we had tried to memorize. Tania said she thought they were taking us to the Central Station. We were a sea of marchers. Tania and I had no possessions; our hands were free. I was walking with a light and bouncy step. Was it fear or the strange parade we were a part of after the weeks spent in cellars? Around us, people were staggering under huge valises; some were transporting a piece of furniture or a rug. Many had children in their arms. Directly in front of us was a man with a large gray-and-red parrot in a cage; every few minutes the bird screamed. The man had the cage door open, and he would put his hand in to quiet the bird.

As in T., when I watched the final departure of the ghetto Jews, but on a vaster scale suited to the breadth of the avenues we were walking on and the enormous length of the column, the crowd was contained on both sides by Ukrainians, SS and Wehrmacht. Many of the Germans were officers. The Ukrainians and their dogs walked with us, while the Germans, immobile on the ruined sidewalks, were like green-and-black statues. From time to time, a Ukrainian would plunge into the column and beat a marcher who was not keeping up with the others or had stopped to shift his load. They beat marchers whose children were crying; we were to make no noise. And they dragged out of the column women who had attracted their attention. They beat them, beat men who tried to shield them, and then led the women to the side, beyond the line held by the Germans. They possessed them singly, in groups, on the ground, leaning them against broken walls of houses. Some women were made to kneel, soldiers holding them from the back by the hair, their gaping mouths entered by penis after penis. Women they had used were pushed back into the column, reeling and weeping, to resume the march. Others were led toward the rubble and bayoneted or shot.

Occasionally, the column halted. Tania and I remained standing; people foolish enough to sit down on a suitcase or a parcel were beaten to the ground and then kicked and shoved till they were properly upright again. During these stops, the selection of women for Ukrainians was most active. Just ahead of us stood a tall and strikingly beautiful young woman with a baby in her arms. I had noticed both her beauty and her elegance; she wore a beige tweed suit with a dark zigzag pattern that reminded me of Tania's old suits. A Ukrainian grabbed her by the arm and was pulling her out of the column. At first she followed without protest, but then she broke away from him and ran toward a German officer standing some two meters away. I had also noticed this officer before. He had a distinguished, placid face and a very fresh uniform. The boots hugging his calves were polished to a high shine that seemed impossible to maintain in this street covered with chalky dust and debris. His arms were crossed on his chest. Could the young woman also have been dazzled by the boots? When she reached the officer, she threw herself on her knees at his feet, held the baby up with one arm, and with the other encircled these superb black tubes. A cloud of annoyance mixed with disdain moved across the officer's face. He gestured for the Ukrainians to stand back; a silence fell as he decided on the correct course of action. What followed the moment of reflection was precise and swift. The officer grasped the child, freed his boots from the young woman's embrace and kicked her hard in the chest. With a step or two he reached an open manhole. There was no lack of these, because the A.K. had used the sewers as routes of attack and escape. He held up the child, looked at it very seriously, and dropped it into the sewer. The Ukrainians took away the mother. In a short while, the column moved forward.

It was late in the afternoon when we reached the great square adjoining the Central Station. The space was divided into two unequal parts. The much larger one was where we and, we supposed, the rest of the remaining population of Warsaw were now gathered. People were lying down, with their heads in the laps of companions; others were sitting on their possessions or crouching on the ground. Alleys kept free for access, like lines of a crossword puzzle, traversed the multitude. On the perimeter Ukrainian guards paced back and forth. The smaller part of the square had become a military encampment, crowded with trucks and armored cars.

Tania and I sat down on the ground, leaning against each other, back to back. Our neighbors, who had been there since the day before, said there was no food and no water to drink except what one could get from people who had a canteen or something to eat in their bundles. Apparently, there was no lack of such clever people among us. We also learned that in the morning and during the previous day parts of the square had been emptied; whole sections had been taken to the station. New arrivals like ourselves had taken their place. The night had been worse than the march and the waiting: the Ukrainians and the Germans were drunk. They roamed through the access alleys, chose women to take to the encampment. There had been screams, probably they tortured as well as raped. Tania asked if anyone knew where the trains would take us. Opinions were divided. Some thought it was just a short ride to some forest where we would be machine-gunned; others talked of concentration camps or work in factories in Germany. Tania also asked about latrines. It turned out there were several points that served that purpose. They were easy to find: one followed the smell. That was, Tania decided, where we would now have to go; we should not wait until the night.

We picked our way among the crowd; there was a long line to use the place. Tania said that after we finished she would somehow buy food and water; we had to keep up our strength. She would do it without me, it would be easier, but first we would choose a place that I would keep for us in one of these clusters. She wanted to find one without crying children or wailing sick: they attracted misfortune. And she wanted us to be in the middle of the group. People trying to be on the outside, to get more air and to be able to get around, were wrong. She didn't care about fresh air; she wanted to live through the night. We did as she said. In a little while she returned. She whispered that she had bread and chocolate. We had not eaten chocolate since the beginning of the uprising. She also had a bottle of water. She had traded her earrings for them; earrings, she informed me, had never been more useful; she had been right to hide them. Best of all, from her point of view, she had also been able to acquire a small mirror, a comb, a lipstick and a blanket. The blanket was for the night, the rest was for the morning. Tania didn't let the food be seen until our neighbors began to eat. She thought it was difficult, and in some degree dangerous, for a woman and a small boy to eat in a hungry crowd without sharing. Then she divided the bread into eve-

ning and morning portions. She allowed us each one
gulp of water. The rest, and especially the chocolate,
were also for the morning. We wrapped ourselves in
the blanket and lay down. It was getting dark; all around
us people were clinging to one another for warmth and
comfort. Tania told me she was afraid of this night, but
we had to make ourselves sleep; if we were exhausted
we would make mistakes. For instance, she said, that
young woman with a child made a terrible mistake when
she knelt down before the officer. She should have stood
as straight as she could, looked him in the eye, and
demanded that he make the Ukrainians behave like dis-
ciplined soldiers. Germans, said Tania, cannot bear the
feeling of pity; they prefer pain. If you ask for pity, you
get the devil that is inside them, worse than the Ukrainians.

The day finally departed. I fell into a dead sleep.
Shouts and curses awoke me. Beams of electric torches
crisscrossed the night. Just as we had been warned,
Ukrainians and Germans were hunting for women. Tania said, Quick, cover me with the blanket and lie on top
of me; pretend I am a bundle. Around us, soldiers were
wading among the sleepers, looking them over, reject-
ing some, hauling away others. Then they were gone.

Peace, disturbed only by sighs, laments and moans
had barely settled on us when we heard a new and im-
probable noise: the loudspeaker the Germans had used
to give orders during the day was now filling the square
with familiar Wehrmacht songs. Some soldier had
brought a gramophone and was playing background
music for a field brothel. But fornication apparently did
not preclude other amusements. Soon, a sound like very
loud static was interfering with the ninth or tenth ren-
dition of ''Lili Marlene.'' It was a machine gun. Cries
of wounded replied. Perhaps a soldier thought it disor-

derly for prisoners to scurry about in the night. The way to end any such unauthorized activity was to aim the fire directly above the heads of people quietly squatting or lying on the ground: anyone who stood up would be mowed down, which was good for discipline. Alas, not everybody could crouch or sit or, better yet, lie facedown. The wounded were begging for help, disembodied voices called for doctors to make themselves known, and doctors who were brave enough to respond became new moving targets.

That night, in turn, departed. It was followed by yet another sparkling and cloudless day. Autumn is the sweetest season in Poland, redolent of harvest smells and promise, a time to pick mushrooms in the moist shade of giant trees. But neither the morning hour nor the season brought with it hope. The loudspeaker began braying lengthy instructions about going to the right and going to the left, forming in groups of fifty, forming in groups of one hundred, leaders responsible for order, picking up trash, sitting, standing and waiting. Since we were thought incapable of comprehending, Ukrainians with their dogs and whips came again into our midst to help us form satisfactory columns. By noon, Tania and I were marching in step in the rear of such a column. The Central Station was before us, oddly unmarked by the fighting. I was very afraid: our destination was about to be revealed.

I could not tell whether Tania was as afraid as I. We had eaten the rest of our bread and chocolate as soon as the sun rose. Unlike most of our neighbors, Tania did not need the help of the Ukrainians to fathom the meaning of the loudspeaker, and the moment it was clear that we were leaving, she had become very busy. Long before the Ukrainians began charging the crowd and one had to stand in ranks at

rigid attention, over my tearful protests she had used
our remaining water to wash our faces and hands. She
brushed the dust off her clothes and mine and
straightened them. Then she combed my hair and,
with great concentration, peering into the pocket
mirror, combed her own hair and put on lipstick,
studied the result, and made little corrections. I was
astonished to see how she had transformed herself.
The stooped-over, soot-smeared old woman of the
march from the Old Town had vanished. Instead,
when we entered the station, I was holding the hand
of a dignified and self-confident young matron. Unlike the day before, she was not hanging back, trying
to lose us in the crowd; she pushed her way to the
outside row and, holding my hand very tight, to my
horror, led me away from the column so that we were
standing, completely exposed, in the space on the
platform between the rest of the people and the train.
Despite my panic, I began to understand that Tania
was putting on a very special show. Her clear blue
eyes surveyed the scene before her; it was as if she
could barely contain her impatience and indignation.
I thought that if she had had an umbrella she would
be tapping the platform with it. And, indeed, what a
tableau was there to contemplate! Two long trains of
cargo and passenger cars, one on each side of the
platform, group after group of Poles in the column
being pushed and beaten by the Ukrainians, then
shoved toward the trains, old people falling on the
platform, some slipping off the platform onto the
tracks as they tried to hoist themselves into the freight
cars, suitcases judged too large by the Ukrainians torn
open and their contents scattered on the ground,
howling dogs pulling on their leashes, Ukrainians

yelling in their mixture of broken Polish and German, people weeping and sometimes embracing each other.

Also surveying the scene, with an air of contempt that matched Tania's indignation, was a fat middle-aged Wehrmacht captain, standing alone a few meters from us, in the middle of the platform. I realized that Tania was including him in her outraged stare and that her show seemed particularly directed at him. All at once, I felt her pulling me behind her again. With a few rapid strides she reached the officer. Addressing him in her haughtiest tone, she asked if he would be kind enough to tell her where these awful trains were going. The answer made my legs tremble: Auschwitz. Completely wrong destination, replied Tania. To find herself with all these disreputable-looking people, being shouted at by drunk and disorderly soldiers, and all this in front of a train going to a place she had never heard of, was intolerable. She was a doctor's wife from R., about two hours from Warsaw; she had come to Warsaw to buy dresses and have her son's eyes examined; of course, everything she bought had been lost in this dreadful confusion. We had nothing to do with whatever was going on here. Would he, as an officer, impose some order and help us find a train to R.? We had spent almost all our money, but she thought she had enough for a second-class compartment. The captain burst out laughing. My dear lady, he said to Tania, not even my wife orders me about quite this way. Could Tania assure him her husband would be glad to have her return? And where had she learned such literary turns of expression? After he had an answer to these basic questions he would see about this wretched train business. Tania blushed. Should I tell you the truth, even though you won't like it? Naturally, replied the captain. I think my husband doesn't mind my being sometimes hot tempered. I learned German in school and probably I managed to improve it by reading, especially everything by Thomas Mann I can find in the original—not much in R., but quite a lot in Warsaw. It's a good way for a provincial housewife to keep occupied. I know Mann's work is forbidden in the Reich, but that is the truth. I am not a party member, merely a railroad specialist, announced the captain still laughing, I am glad you have chosen a great stylist. Shall I get someone to carry your suitcases while we look for transportation to R.?

The captain was a man of the world. He did not feel compelled to introduce himself and gave no sign of being discouraged or startled by our lack of luggage. Having handed Tania into a first-class compartment of a train waiting at a distant platform, he clicked his heels. Tania was not to worry. He was signing a pass to R.; it was not necessary to buy tickets; the German reservist in charge of this military train would see to it that she was not disturbed.

The train remained in the station for some hours after he left us. Slowly, it filled up with soldiers; noisy groups of officers were in the compartments on both sides of ours. Meanwhile, Tania's excitement left her and with it her boldness: her face turned haggard, it was the face of the night before. She could not stop shivering or talking about our being doomed because the train had not left. She was sure the captain would mention the amusing little shrew from R. with an interest in Mann to some officer whose understanding extended beyond railway trains, and they would immediately send the Gestapo to get us. Once again, she had gone too far with her lies; we would pay for it. But no one came. The officers who glanced at us curiously as they passed in the corridor continued on their way. A whistle blew, the train started, and soon the elderly reservist came to tell us that the next stop would be G., more than halfway to R.

VI

THE FIELDS WERE VERY FLAT. AT THE EDGE OF THE horizon one could distinguish a line of trees, probably similar to the parallel line of trees near us that marked the western boundary of the pastures belonging to the village of Piasowe. To the right and left were other lines of demarcation: rutted passages, made by cart wheels and hooves of horses and cattle, running in an almost straight line to that western boundary, just wide enough for a cart; and elsewhere long, thin, grass-covered mounds separating a peasant's land from that of his neighbor. Farther off to the right, at a distance of some three kilometers, there was the dirt highway with which the main road of Piasowe made a right angle. Peasants' horse-drawn carts moved along it, sometimes at a brisk trot when the cart was empty and the peasant cracked his whip, and sometimes at a pace so slow that a good part of the day was gone before the cart disappeared from view. Once in a long while, rarely enough to provoke comment in the village, a German truck or staff car would pass, enveloped in a cloud of white dust. The highway led west to Rawa; to the east lay W., where the market was held, and, much farther, G. Beyond the highway was the forest. At this time of the year all the crops were in, and the passages between the fields were used mostly to haul hay from distant stacks to the barns.

Returning to the stables in the evening, we would

drive our cows along these passages, together with other children from Piasowe who grazed cattle in adjoining pastures. We could get the cows home more quickly that way than through the fields, without making them run, which was bad for the milk and sometimes even dangerous for the cows. The cows liked having a path to follow. It was also more fun for us, because it made a large herd of cattle, cows lowing and jostling one another. There were four of us who took cows to the same pasture, two other boys and a girl; the houses we belonged to stood in a clump with their outbuildings; the other houses of Piasowe were up the village road, closer to the highway. The barns and stables gave onto the fields directly; the houses were separated from them by large yards. Perpendicular to each house, on one side of the yard, were usually pigsties and chicken coops, and on the other side manure piles. The houses faced the village road; their outbuildings were enclosed by wooden fences to keep the poultry and piglets inside during the day. At night, the dogs would be off the chain: the fences kept them in too.

We children were responsible for some twenty cows and heifers. Three of the cows belonged to Tania's and my master, a slow-talking bald peasant called Kula. The cows grazed peacefully, picking at the stubble; when Stefa told us it was time, we would move them, calling them by their names and waving the stripped branches we used to poke at them and hit them. At thirteen, Stefa was the oldest. The boys were my age. We always did what Stefa said when it came to taking care of the cows. In fact, there was not much to do, besides changing every couple of hours from a place that was overgrazed and making sure the heifers did not wander off. The cows were content to eat and chew and drop turds; we brought excitement into their lives only occasionally, when Stefa agreed that a little running early in the day would do them no great harm. Then we would give one another boosts to get on a cow's back and try to ride her in a circle around the herd. Sometimes even Stefa would take a turn. She usually managed to stay on the longest.

Our serious business was to keep from freezing. There were no trees in the pasture and no dead branches to burn. We made fires out of a few dry cow turds and sat cross-legged around them. At noon, we would scratch a hole in the ground, put our potatoes in it, and cover them with dirt. Then we pushed the fire right over the potatoes. We would build the fire up to make it really strong, still trying not to use many turds because very dry ones were hard to find. In about an hour, the meal would be ready. Somebody always brought salt. The baked potatoes would make warmth circulate from the stomach throughout the body. They thawed out our hands. We would eat two or three potatoes and wish we had more.

We used a little hay from a nearby haystack to start our fires; it reminded me of dry flower stalks and the game my grandfather had played with Zosia and me in our garden. I told Stefa and the boys that we could make fires to jump over. They wanted to try it. The next day, we brought bundles of straw under our jackets and arranged the fires in a row, close together, so that as soon as one had jumped over a fire one had to leap into the next one. The straw burned with a quick hot flame; they liked the game, although we didn't have enough straw to make it last long. We began to play almost every day. Running and jumping helped warm us.

I realized that jumping over fires, which I had taught them, was the only game they knew. They liked to ride the cows, to hit a crow with a stone, or to grab a cat by the tail and whirl it, but that did not seem to me to be playing; it was real teasing and hurting, more like catching a hen in the yard, holding it with one hand by the wings and, with the other, wringing its neck. I could not deny that I enjoyed watching a hen killed this way. The hen would flap its wings and try to fly and skid when it was running away and make a huge cackling sound once it was caught; even Kula and his wife, Kulowa, laughed each time they saw it. But it had nothing to do with pretending. I told Stefa and the boys about how I had played when I was little—only I didn't say it was in T., because T. was none of their business—in the sandbox in the courtyard of our house, or on the swing and the slide that were attached to the jungle gym, or on the jungle gym itself. I drew pictures of this equipment in the dirt with my finger. Such stories made them cover their mouths with their hands and giggle; they didn't say I was lying, they said I was crazy. Who would ever make a pile of sand for a child to throw around or pour water into? That would just make a mess. These other things, nobody had ever seen them or anything like them; there had never been any talk of jungle gyms in Piasowe.

As I told them about Warsaw, where I said we had once lived, its tall buildings, trolley cars, automobiles, electric lights and radios, their wonder grew, and so did mine. I found that only Stefa had ever been to another village, one just like Piasowe but a long walk past the line of horizon we stared at all day, because that was where her mother's parents lived. The others had never gone beyond the line of trees at the end of the fields of Piasowe or the end of the village road, where it met the highway. That is why the line of the horizon was so mysterious; neither they nor I knew what was hidden

beyond it. I knew about Rawa only as a name: Tania
had told me that was where the highway led if one traveled on it more than fifty kilometers past Piasowe; it
had a railroad station. I knew about G. and W. because
Tania and I had passed through them.

Stefa and the boys liked to listen to me, especially
after I learned to avoid talking about things that bothered them by being strange instead of amusing. The
uprising in Warsaw interested them—I disregarded Tania's orders and talked about it; they knew about guns
and about fighting between the Germans and the partisans. There were partisans in the forest. Once, during
the previous summer, German soldiers tried to get the
partisans there but failed and afterward went through
the village looking for any who might be hiding with
the peasants. But none were found, so the Germans just
took away all the sausages and bacon they saw, and the
partisans were still in the forest. Sometimes they came
out at night and raided the village, also to get food.
Stefa said they could be worse than the Germans: they
were after women as well as food.

I liked to listen to their stories about Piasowe. According to them, only Komar, the rich peasant who sold
vodka at the entrance of the village, could read a little
and, some people said, knew how to count better than
any town person. Nobody in Piasowe had been to
school; W. was too far. The idea of going to school
instead of working in the fields or with the animals made
them giggle. The priest came to Piasowe from W. every
few weeks to baptize, marry and celebrate Mass. He
had given them Communion.

They talked about Kula and Kulowa. I knew, of
course, that Kula's son Tadek was the butcher for all of
Piasowe and the adjoining villages, in addition to helping his father with the land. They said Kula was afraid

of Tadek, although he was himself very strong. When Tadek was drunk, he beat his parents, especially Kulowa. Once he knocked out Kula's teeth. They fought because Kula would not divide his land so Tadek could marry. They advised me to stay out of Tadek's way. He would leave Tania alone: it didn't matter that she now worked as Kula's servant; she was still a schoolteacher. The Kula daughter, Masia, they all liked, as did Tania and I. This gay and round-faced girl used to take Kula's cows to pasture until Kula got Stefa to help out. Masia too wanted to get married, and Kula wouldn't hear of it and whipped her every time she talked to him about it. He preferred to keep her at home, so she would work, and he didn't want to give her a dowry. Still, Stefa's brother, Jurek, really wanted to marry her, and Jurek put it into her in Kula's barn every Sunday and whenever else they had a chance, to get Masia pregnant. Then Kula would have to give them permission. Tadek liked to watch. They did it in a corner so that Tadek and some of his friends could climb to the hayloft from the outside and see everything. Kula and Kulowa were probably the only two people in Piasowe who didn't know what was going on.

Stefa said it was no wonder Kula had hired Tania when we arrived: Kula had so much land that getting in the potatoes and beets on time was too much even for the four Kulas. Somebody had to do the rest of the work, taking the cows to pasture, milking, feeding the poultry and the pigs. Now Kula might begin to ask himself whether, with Tania doing so much of the work in the house, Masia wouldn't get lazy and run after Jurek even more. I was another matter; having Masia instead of me go out with the cows was a waste, and he didn't like paying Stefa's father to have her do it.

I would tell these things to Tania when we lay down

for the night on our straw mattress and began listening to Kula and Kulowa snore in the next room, like peasants sawing logs, and Masia's gentler and more regular noise. Tania said she had already considered the problem and was making her plans.

We had been in Piasowe almost two months. On the train from Warsaw to R., Tania had grown increasingly nervous. Fortunately, it seemed that the Wehrmacht captain had not spoken to anyone about us before the train left the station, but it was only a matter of time before he talked, and then they would telephone the Gestapo in R. We would be picked up as soon as we got off the train. And why R., why had she said we were from R.? R. was much too big, really a little city, it would be full of Polish and German police. They would check our papers at the station, and how was she going to explain why we were traveling from Warsaw to R. instead of Auschwitz? We must get off at the next stop, G. She had never heard of G., so it must be small, perhaps without any police at the station. Also, if she was right, and the captain had talked by now, it was unlikely they would be looking for us in G. But we wouldn't get off the train until it began to pull out of the G. station; that way the German reservist wouldn't have an opportunity to interfere even if he was surprised we were not continuing to R. and became suspicious. We would simply wait near the railroad-car door, as though we were getting a breath of fresh air.

Tania was right. We left the train in G. unhindered. There were no policemen on the platform or in the station; outside, the town seemed asleep or deserted. We went into the first restaurant we saw. Tania asked for soup and bread; I was so hungry that the smell of the potato soup made me feel weak. The serving girl who took the order disappeared into the kitchen. Through the open door, we heard her talk and a man's voice answer. The soup turned out to be wonderfully thick and hot. It burned its way down my throat to my stomach.

Before we finished eating, a man came out of the kitchen, said he was the owner, and very politely asked if he could sit down with us. Tania told him he was welcome and began to talk quickly about how good the soup tasted. He interrupted her with a smile; there were more serious matters he needed to discuss with her. He could see at a glance we had somehow managed to get out of Warsaw but wasn't sure we understood what kind of danger we were in. The Germans had published orders not only to the police but to the entire population that refugees from Warsaw were to be turned over to the German police. Of course, we were not the first refugees to have reached G. Most had come at the beginning of August; apparently they had more or less walked out of the city and made their way here. Lately, there had been very few. He didn't know what happened to the ones the Germans got. They were not seen again. He was going to help us, that was his responsibility, but the organization had limited means. All they could do was give us some clothes and find a peasant with a horse and cart to take us as far away from G. as the peasant could be persuaded to go. Then we would be on our own. But all that could wait until the morning. For the moment, we should eat all we could hold and then get a good sleep.

While we had more soup and later fried eggs with kielbasa, Tania and our host kept talking. She told him about the fighting during the last weeks in Warsaw and how we escaped. He explained about the Mazowsze, the region we were in. There were villages in this part of the country so remote and isolated—he hoped to send us to one of them—that they might as well be in another world. If Germans went there, it was to confiscate horses or pigs, not to check documents. The peasants had not changed in the last hundred years. They didn't know that taking in refugees from Warsaw was forbidden or that money could be made blackmailing them. Probably not too many of them even knew there was such a place as Warsaw. But Tania didn't need to feel guilty about the peasants: our presence wouldn't be a danger for them. There weren't enough Germans to look for refugees in those villages, where the devil wishes you good-night. He thought Tania might tell the peasants that we had run away from the Russian front—no use giving details, since they wouldn't understand and wouldn't care—that she was a schoolteacher, which ought to win her some respect, and that for lodging and food we were willing to work as farm servants until the war was over. We were lucky, because peasants were now digging up potatoes and soon would be digging beets; they needed all the help they could get. Once that work was finished the peasant we were living with might not want to go on feeding extra mouths, but the war was ending, and, besides, by that time Tania would know more about Mazowsze peasants than he.

We went to bed happy. For the first time in two months we didn't have the sound of gunfire in our ears. We were in a dry warm attic above the restaurant, in a real bed. A friend was looking after us.

Our host awakened us at dawn; he wanted us out of G. before Polish police or German patrols appeared on the road leading out of the town. The peasant who agreed to take us in his cart was willing to go quite a long distance west, beyond W. He had in mind a village where he often delivered *samogon*, home-distilled vodka. That village turned out to be Piasowe. Like most peasant carts, his was a long contraption with four high wheels, pulled by a single horse. The bottom was made of three wide boards. The sides were ladders fixed at a wide angle to the bottom. The peasant sat on a board fixed across the ladders. There was some hay in the cart on which Tania and I stretched out. It was a very good feeling to have taken a bath and be wearing clean clothes. Our stomachs were full; we looked at fields and stands of trees slowly going past us. We were not particularly afraid. Our host had given us some bread and cheese to take along for a second breakfast. We decided to eat it right away. The peasant kept his horse going at a good pace, as though he had been schooled by my grandfather. A couple of times he stopped to urinate at the side of the road. He asked if we also wanted to relieve ourselves; Tania's continence amused him.

We rolled on. When W. appeared in the distance, he slowed down and explained that he was going to leave the highway to avoid going through the town. He would take advantage of the detour to feed the horses and get something to eat for himself and for us. After traveling a considerable distance over lanes just wide enough for the cart, we turned into a village and then into a farm-yard. A great deal of persuasion was needed to quiet the dogs so that Tania and I were able to get off and eat more bread and cheese and drink buttermilk. Our peasant talked to his friends and then lay down in the barn for a loud nap. The sun began to seem low to Tania. She roused the peasant, and soon we were on the road again. Night was falling when we arrived in Piasowe at the house of the peasant called Komar, on whom Tania concentrated all her charm. She wanted him to help us get established in the village.

Komar was the entrepreneur of Piasowe. His two sons-in-law helped with the land and left him free to run his businesses, the most important being the little shop in his house from which he sold wares like salt, matches and nails. The principal merchandise, however, was vodka, or *samogon* passing for vodka, or *samogon* undisguised. Liquor could be bought by the bottle, when a peasant felt ready to pay for a night of oblivion, or consumed more modestly by the glass on Komar's premises in the company of neighbors. It was Komar who drove grain to the mill and brought back flour. He took potatoes, beets, butter and cheese to the market in W. and came back with town goods that he had bought or bartered on order. There were other householders in Piasowe who had horses—they used them to work their fields and also the fields of others for pay or in exchange for help with the harvest—but in addition to his pair of horses, Komar had a head for figures, and felt none of the disquiet that possessed the other peasants at the thought of trotting down the highway, away from Piasowe. For a long moment it seemed as though Komar would become our employer: Tania was proposing to keep his books, sell his vodka and, in her spare time, teach his grandchildren. Then Komar changed his mind: too many people passed through his place every day, and they were not always peasants. Old Kula was the man; he needed help with the harvest. Komar would take us to him.

Kula and his family had finished the day's work when we entered their house, preceded by Komar. They were in a large kitchen, about to eat the evening meal. Tania and I stood in the door while Komar greeted the Kulas, inquired about the progress of the harvest and then

talked about us. I looked around the kitchen, trying
not to turn my head. The floor was made of very white
planks, the table was a long rectangle of dark wood.
The walls were whitewashed; near the door opposite
us that seemed to lead from the kitchen to the yard
hung a black icon, a copy of the Virgin of
Częstochowa. A naphtha lamp stood on the table, its
wick turned up to throw a large round of yellow light.
A candle was burning in a holder nailed to the wall
under the icon.

Having listened to Komar's explanation, Kula got up
and looked us over carefully and unsmilingly. Tania apparently understood what was disturbing him and took
the initiative. She bowed to him and in the direction of
Kulowa and said that they must not worry about our
being city people, unable to work hard. She was healthy
and strong. I was a well-behaved and obedient boy. If
they took us in, and showed us how to do the tasks that
were to be done, we would not let them down and God
would repay their kindness. She was not asking for
wages; just a corner of the kitchen where we might
sleep and a place at their table. After a lengthy silence,
during which Tadek and Masia also got up to gape at
us, Kula nodded agreement. Kulowa motioned for us
to sit down on the bench beside her, Masia brought
plates and spoons for our soup and boiled potatoes,
Kula got a bottle of vodka and filled glasses for himself,
Tadek and Komar. The deal was done.

Inspired by Tania's example, I seized Kulowa's fore-
arm with both hands and deposited a slow and cere-
monious kiss on her elbow. My readings in Sieńkiewicz
had taught me that this was an ancient Polish gesture
of respect. I could not have aimed better. Kulowa may
have been more surprised than moved, but she embraced me and became a shield against Kula's bad tem-

per. After the third glass of vodka, Komar left. It was
time to settle for the night. Kulowa produced a huge
burlap sack and sent Masia to the barn to fill it with
straw. When that was done, she showed Tania how to
sew its end closed so it would become our mattress,
and she gave us a feather bed to sleep under. Masia
brought her bedding from the only other room in the
house, where she told me the parents slept, and put
it on the floor near the stove. We would be against
the wall, on the other side of the kitchen. During these
preparations, Tadek left. I asked Masia where he slept.
She giggled. Tadek liked to be near the animals. He
slept in the hayloft, above the cows. One other arrangement remained to be made: Kula said he would
leave the dog on the chain this first night. When we
needed to relieve ourselves, we could go behind the
barn.

To harvest the potatoes, one dug around them first
with a hoe. When the soil was sufficiently loosened,
one could pull them up with one's hands. The next step
was to throw the potatoes into a basket. Then one
lugged the basket to the lane between the fields, where
the cart would eventually come, and heaped the potatoes on a big pile. When Kula stopped the cart next to
the pile, the potatoes were loaded on by hand or with
a pitchfork. The piles had to be large enough so that
Kula's time would not be wasted; he didn't want to
make too many stops. Tania and Masia hoed and pulled
up the potatoes, and I put them in the basket and stag-
gered with it to the piles. When I fell behind, they would
stop their work and help me. Soon Tania's hands were
badly blistered. Masia gave her strips of cloth to tie
around them. I tried to use the hoe in Tania's place, but
I was not strong enough to go fast.

We needed to hurry because the beets had to be done next and sent to W. before there was any risk that they might freeze. On the other hand, if they were taken out of the ground too early, warm weather would make them ferment. At noon, Kulowa came into the field with boiled potatoes and buttermilk. Afterward, we worked again until dusk. It took many days to finish the potatoes. Then came time for Kula's beets. Tania's blisters had broken; hard calluses replaced them. When we lay down at night, she would ask me to rub her back as long as I could stand it. She said that in the field she sometimes thought she could never straighten herself again. Our shoes disintegrated. Tania bought wooden clogs from Komar. We learned to wear them like everybody else in Piasowe.

Kula decided that Masia did not need both Tania and me for the potatoes; I would go out with the cows so he would no longer have to pay Stefa's father to have her look after them. Stefa showed me how to get the cows out of their stalls in the morning, after Masia had milked them, and get them moving in the direction of the rest of the herd. In the beginning, I was scared of the cows but managed to hide my fear enough so that Stefa and the boys wouldn't despise me. Also, I was repelled by the sight and smell of manure in the barn and in the yard and the globs of dung that stuck to the cows' sides. When we gathered turds for our fire, I dreaded mistakenly picking up one that was not dry underneath and getting my fingers covered with dung. Quite soon, I learned that Kula's cows were lazy and pacific; I also found out which of the other cows were bad tempered and learned to watch out for their horns.

As we burned our turd fires and played tricks on the cows, I began to feel that being dirty and touching dirt conferred on me a sort of freedom. In the pasture, Stefa would hitch up her skirt, the rest of us would let down our pants, and we would squat down to defecate where we happened to be. If our own turds were not perfectly formed or were too wet, and we felt the need of a wipe, it was accomplished with a handful of dry stubble. Without asking Tania, I came to the conclusion that the children I was with were not on the lookout for circumcised penises. Nonetheless, when I took out mine, as often as possible I would hold it by the end to conceal my lack of a foreskin. In the stable, I was cleaning out the stalls and pitchforking manure with enthusiasm and results that were sufficient for Kula not to comment about my work. One day, I drove the pitchfork into my foot. It made a nasty puncture wound that Tania tried to open so it would bleed better. She could not remember when I had last had a tetanus injection and was wild with worry. The wound healed normally while I hobbled around after the cows and did my chores.

Soon I was able to terrorize Tania with another medical problem. For some time, we had been trying, when we were out with the cows, to smoke a mixture of dry leaves, hay and grass in a pipe that belonged to one of the boys. That led to nothing more than attacks of coughing and a burning throat. One day, Stefa got hold of a package of cigarette tobacco, which must have been of the lowest and strongest grade obtainable, tobacco then sold in Poland being, in any event, vile. We smoked this stuff as long as it lasted. When it was time to drive the cows home, I was desperately sick. I rubbed my face and hands with cow dung to mask the smell of tobacco; the stench of vomit complemented my efforts. The vomiting was followed by diarrhea that continued through the night and into the next day. I was green; my teeth chattered; I was unable to eat. Just as Tania came close to concluding I had come down with typhoid fever, I miraculously recovered. Nothing could induce me to reveal to her the true nature of my illness.

In part this was because of Tania's severity and particular methods of punishment. I understood her insistence on perfect behavior, or in any event behavior that corresponded to what she wanted, when the outside world was concerned. One could say that our lives depended on it. But she was equally insistent on my controlling myself and being controlled by her at times when I thought it didn't matter, when we were alone. It may be that she thought I needed to be in constant training. More likely, it was because of the effort she was making never to lose the complete hold she had on herself and because we were constantly together. Already in T., after we had moved to our new lodgings with Pan and Pani Kramer, we slept in the same room. That stopped when we went to the apartment in Lwów that Reinhard had found. Since the day of his death, however, we had spent each night in the same bed. Some of these beds were narrow, often narrower than the straw mattress we now shared in Kula's kitchen, where Masia's presence on her mattress diluted our intimacy, and the rooms were themselves exiguous, yet I had never seen Tania naked. Tania undressed was Tania in her slip or Tania in her long nightgown. Her bodily functions were private, even under the most constraining conditions. On the other hand, my nakedness and my bowel and bladder movements continued to be subject to question, inspection and comment.

Never being alone, always being with Tania, had begun in Lwów because Reinhard came only on week-

ends. The meals and discussions with our fellow lodgers at Pani Dumont's were part of the joint performance
we were required to give. Pani Bronicka occasionally
insisted that Tania leave the room so that I would be,
as she put it, less subject to telepathy, but most of the
time she wouldn't say anything and Tania would remain, her eyes on the pages of a book but in reality
listening to every word that was said and noting each
one of my gestures. The great exceptions were the hours
we spent with my grandfather, when Tania's attention and
supervision weakened like a magnet shedding pins or
nails, and the afternoons of catechism. With Father P. and
his class, I was certainly putting on a show for which
Tania had rehearsed me in detail, but still it was I who
was putting it on, and my performance was unsuper-
vised. Otherwise, for years it had been as Tania pre-
dicted: a day-and-night partnership of Tania and Maciek
contra mundum, with the world against us. And I admired and loved my beautiful and brave aunt with increasing passion. Her body could never be close enough
to mine; she was the fortress against danger and the
well of all comfort; regardless of the circumstances,
whether it was her nightgown not having dried or, as
now at Kula's, her no longer owning a nightgown, I
waited impatiently for the nights when I knew she would
come to bed wearing only a slip so that I could feel
closer to her.

During those years, when each word that she said
or that was said to her had to be examined for dangers
it might provoke or portend, Tania's speech and gestures, except to my grandfather and me, were never
without purpose. That purpose was to conceal and
please, to concentrate attention on what might gratify
the listener and deflect it from us. I played the sup-
porting role. With me she made no effort to be pleas-

ant; that was natural enough, and I think I did not expect anything else. But for Tania, the distinction between lack of pretense and harshness scarcely existed. Each fault of my conduct or appearance, so long as we were alone, which as I have said was almost always, became the subject of unrestrained, precise and critical comment. In a way, it was as if one performer were speaking to another about their art. And if she found my reaction to her observations foolish, or if whatever she was commenting on had really given her cause for annoyance, Tania would fall silent; she had a face of dolorous stone. Her silence could last hours or days depending on the gravity of the offense she had perceived and my pleas for forgiveness. Of course, since we were performers, the show had to go on: an immediate truce would apply, and criticisms or silence were replaced by cloying sweetness as soon as we had an audience.

But now, at Piasowe and under Kula's roof, we were differently situated. Every day I got up at dawn to help Masia or Kulowa milk the cows, and then I disappeared, taking the cows to pasture and returning with them just in time for the evening milking. Then, immediately, there was mash to be taken to the pigs or possibly something urgent to be done about the hens. Sitting at last beside Tania for the evening meal, with both elbows on the table, I would eat my soup as noisily as Tadek. Tania could not reprove me, although I knew that each slurp plunged a knife into her heart. That would have been an indirect criticism of Tadek and, as such, against her rules. In total contrast with our life in Lwów and Warsaw, in Piasowe we were never alone except at night; once the soft drone of Masia's snoring became regular, we would whisper, holding each other tight under the feather bed as long as we could hold out against

fatigue and sleepiness, but that was a time to share secrets and caresses, and not a time for Tania to be angry.
And Tania could not punish me by silence; that would
have been putting on a wrong sort of show for the Kulas. It was thus possible that I could have told Tania the
truth, and that my unsuccessful introduction to tobacco
would have only made her laugh and kiss me and say I
was just like my grandfather. But fear of Tania's punishments was only a part of what held me back with
such force from confessing and made me prefer to in-
crease her suffering as well as my own. I was chained
to the habit of lying, and I no longer believed that weak-
ness or foolishness or mistakes could be forgiven by
Tania or by me.

The principal secret we were discussing those nights
was Tania's business venture with Komar. As soon as
the potatoes and beets were done and her work changed
to lighter chores, like churning cream to make butter,
washing the kitchen floor, doing the laundry, and preparing the feed for the poultry, she noticed, just as Stefa
had foretold, that Kula was throwing increasingly cross
looks in her direction. She took to visiting Komar before the evening meal; her work was now finished early
enough to allow it. Komar talked to her about the war.
His network of commercial relations was a source of
unending astonishment, as was the information it
brought him. She learned that the Russians were in
Czechoslovakia and had crossed the Danube, the Americans and the English were almost on the Rhine; the
Germans were beaten and except for us the war was
practically over.

She drank with Komar. Her ability to down anything
he poured, crack jokes, and distinguish among the
grades of his vodka and *samogon* impressed him. This

schoolteacher had uncommon gifts; he told her he regretted not having kept her instead of sending us to that old fool Kula. In turn, she explained how precarious her position with Kula had become: she was wondering how many days it would be before he threw her and her son out to beg on the highway or look for the partisans in the forest. Komar grew dark with anger at the thought; indignation was father to a business proposition. With Christmas approaching, the peasants' demand for vodka was overwhelming him. Would she become his saleswoman and courier? He would pay a commission and make an immediate advance against future earnings. Thus she could pay Kula for her lodging, I would continue to mind the cows, and we would all live happily until the Russians came and robbed us. They drank bottoms up to toast Komar's plans. The next day, Komar called on Kula as we were eating our supper, a bottle of vodka in the pocket of his sheepskin coat. Such doubts as Kula might have initially had about letting us stay on were washed away. Before we went to sleep, Tania made her bargain with him about the money.

"*Bimber*" was the wartime name for illegal, home-distilled vodka. This substance was not without danger to the drinker; lower grades caused blindness and paralysis. Manufacturers and sellers were preyed upon by the police, who did not permit the imminent collapse of established order to interfere with their enforcement, mostly through blackmail, of the state liquor monopoly. Small wonder, therefore, that the business was run from the top by big city slickers, *cwaniaki*, refugees from Warsaw, spreading out from G. into the countryside of the Mazowsze. Tania became Komar's emissary to these dealers. She traveled to W. once a week in Komar's cart to pick up the merchandise. Then she would visit,

at first with Komar and later alone, peasants in villages
near Piasowe who ran establishments similar to Komar's, and offer her wares to them. The key to a sale
was a sufficient level of confidence: the peasant had to
feel certain that the *bimber* he was buying was safe to
drink. Nothing built confidence more quickly than having the supplier down a glass of the liquor right under
the buyer's watchful gaze, certifying in this manner each
bottle. Tania could sample as many bottles as she had
the strength to carry, and still have the wits to drive a
hard bargain on price and rush back to Komar for more
bottles to carry to the next village. At first she trudged
from village to village in her wooden clogs; quickly she
was able to buy for herself knee-high leather boots, the
mark of a successful black-market operator, and for me
real shoes. Komar had been right about demand. Soon
it was necessary to go to W. as often as every other day
and sometimes to use the horse and cart for deliveries.
It helped that Tania became friendly with the principal
dealer, Pan Nowak. Now, when *bimber* was scarce,
there was always enough for Tania and Komar. While
Komar or his son-in-law took care of the horses and
loaded the cart, Tania and Nowak discussed news from
the front and speculated about when the Russians would
attack again in Poland and in which direction they would
strike.

Pan Nowak complained about being alone in W. with
nobody to talk to except peasants and small-town ig-
noramuses; if Pani would only leave Piasowe, they
could work together and make a fortune before the war
ended. There wasn't a village within a hundred kilometers in any direction from W. where he didn't deal
with the peasant who sold vodka and had the whole
village under his thumb.

Tania told me that Nowak's intentions were not confined to marketing *bimber* and having someone intelligent to talk to, and she decided she would flirt with him just a little, for the good of the business, even though he was a repulsive gangster. She was also using him for another purpose. Since he had all these connections, she gave him the name that grandfather had used in Warsaw and his description. Nowak swore to ask each of his peasants if there was such a man in his village. One could not tell; perhaps grandfather was somewhere near us; there seemed to be so many refugees from Warsaw in this wilderness. She had a feeling we could find him through Nowak. Finding my grandfather became a continuous and overwhelming fantasy for both of us. We would whisper about it at night, between anecdotes of *bimber* sales and Kula's moods and Tania's worried questions about my staying warm in the pasture. She wanted to get a sheepskin jacket for me, but they were hard to find; besides, I didn't want one. I wanted to be dressed like the others, in layers of patched, cast-off coats, to look like a scarecrow.

Light snow fell several times, but the cows could still graze. It was so cold in the pasture that we had to keep moving and stamping our feet, our arms crossed on our chests and hands buried in the sleeves. Kulowa wanted to start preparations for Christmas. Kula agreed and told Tadek to slaughter the biggest pig, a muddy, suspicious-looking animal. Kula didn't intend to keep all the meat for himself; he would sell most of it in the village and to Komar.

Neighbors came to help and watch. First, they got the pig into the yard with pitchforks. He stood there grunting. A few times, he made a sudden rush to get away, but they always drove him back into the center.

Then it was Tadek and Kula and Stefa's brother, Jurek, who rushed the pig, stood him upright and tied him to a post. He was squealing now, the neighbors were pricking him with their pitchforks, and the other pigs in the pigsty were making a terrible noise. Everybody was joking that the pig must have been through this before to be so scared, and what a pity it was he would not be eating his own ham. Meanwhile Tadek got his knives and a big basin that he gave to Kulowa to hold. When he slit the pig's throat, it made a coughing noise, and blood gushed so strongly that Kulowa had trouble catching it all in the basin. After they decided that the pig had done all his bleeding, Tadek shaved parts of him and skinned the others and, slicing very fast, began to separate the different cuts. Once in a while, he would throw a piece he didn't want to the dog, who was dancing wildly on his hind legs, head held back by the chain. The dog's antics began to annoy Tadek. He went over to the dog, a piece of meat in his hand, and when the dog opened his mouth to take it, he kicked him in the stomach. That made the dog crawl into his house and Tadek began to tease him. He would hold out a scrap, the dog would rush for it, and sometimes Tadek gave it to him and sometimes he kicked him or hit him with a meat mallet he had taken in his other hand and hid behind his back. This game went on for a long time, because the dog did not seem to catch on or know what to expect.

The women were in the kitchen, chopping and grinding meat for sausages. When he finished playing with the dog, Tadek set up the machine for stuffing sausage skins and got a couple of the women started on it. They made blood sausages first, having set aside just enough blood for the soup. Kula and the other men were drinking in the yard, passing the bottle from hand to hand.

They became very loud. When the bottle was empty, Kula called to Tania and asked what was the use of having her and her bastard in the house if she did not even offer them a bottle of *bimber* when she saw that his bottle was dry. Tania thought that over and answered she wasn't in the business of offering vodka to him any more than he was in the business of offering hospitality to her and her son. Still, she would give him one bottle if he bought two. That made the other peasants laugh and clap Kula on the back saying that the scythe had struck a hard stone. Kula began to laugh too and said he meant no offense. Tania held out her hand for him to shake, said she never stopped being grateful to him and the mistress, and went to Komar's to get the bottles.

Meanwhile the soup and the plates of cubed bacon, fried until it rendered all the lard, had been set out, ready to eat. Even the children were given big slices of bread to eat with the bacon or dip into the boiling fat. A chorus of joyful shouts greeted the arrival of Tania with a bottle, which she immediately uncorked and handed to Kula. Behind her were Komar and another man I didn't know, wearing high leather boots like Tania's and a rich sheepskin coat that met his boot tops. Tania called me over and made the introduction. It was Nowak. He pinched my ear. Passing near Piasowe, he explained, he could not help dropping in on his friend Komar, and now he was lucky also to see the most beautiful woman of Warsaw. By pure chance, he had some trifles for us. He gave Tania a package with a red woolen scarf in it, which she immediately tied around her shoulders. While she was inspecting the effect in the mirror in the Kulas' room, Nowak pinched my ear some more and gave me a large mouth harmonica. That was a present I was really glad to receive. As soon as

Tania gave me permission, I said good-bye to Nowak and went to the barn with Stefa and the boys to try it out.

They drank until late. Nowak borrowed my harmonica; it turned out he could play very well. First, Tania and Komar danced. Then Komar played and Nowak danced with Tania. They even got Kula to dance with Kulowa and later with Tania. Stefa told me that the show in the barn had begun. Jurek and Masia were hard at it and Tadek was watching. Komar and Nowak brought more bottles. Many of the peasants were very drunk; they would rush out of the kitchen to vomit in the yard, stagger back, and, after eating a piece of bread with lard, drink again. Nowak wanted to show Tania the hat on the head of the man in the moon. This took quite a while. When they returned, Tania looked very serious. Then a second round of bottles was drunk. Tania alone still seemed sober. The peasants were being dragged home by their wives. Shaking with hiccups, Nowak addressed long and gallant remarks to Tania, all about the absolute urgency of meeting again before the week was out. Then he and Komar also left.

When we went to bed that night, Tania told me not to pester her about Nowak's man in the moon. Nowak had used the pretext about the man in the moon to be able to speak to her alone. She knew how to handle Nowak and would continue to handle him as long as it suited her. The important thing was that perhaps he had found grandfather. A peasant he had talked to a few days ago told him he had heard there was an older Pan, with a name that could be the right one, in a neighboring village. That Pan came in almost every day to have a glass or two of vodka with the man who sold vodka there. The name of the village was Bieda,

less than thirty kilometers from Piasowe. It could all
be a mistake, but she didn't think so. She had decided
how she would get there. Hiring a peasant with a horse
and cart in Piasowe was out of the question. There
were too many risks, whether it turned out to be
grandfather or not. She didn't want every gossip in
Piasowe and Bieda involved in our affairs. Instead, she
would start out on foot in the morning, before anybody else woke up. If she was lucky, she would find
a peasant on the road to Bieda who would give her a
lift. She would worry about how to get back once she
was in Bieda; the only thing that mattered was that
this man should turn out to be grandfather. It was impossible to let me come with her; I would slow her
down.

I saw that her mind was made up and asked what I
should say to Kula or Komar if they asked where she
was. Tania had not thought about this. First she told
me not to worry, nobody would ask, because she
would have returned to Piasowe before I brought the
cows back from the pasture. Later, when I was almost
asleep, she said it would be best to pretend I knew
nothing; let them guess she had gone to meet Nowak.
She was too tired to think, but on her way back to
Piasowe she would decide what story to tell, depending on whether she had found grandfather and what he
thought she should do. After that, we tried to sleep,
but we slept very little, we were so full of hope and
so frightened. It was still dark when Tania tiptoed
barefoot out of the kitchen. The dog recognized her;
he made no noise.

The day passed slowly. Stefa said it was going to
snow, but it didn't. It just got colder and windier. All
the good of our fire seemed to disappear in the gale.
An old cow, almost entirely black, with heavy eyes,

was my favorite. She liked being scratched and talked to. I would put my arms around her neck and stand for a long time pressed against her flank. When the warmth of her body had penetrated mine, I would go back to Stefa and the boys and our fire. We talked about the pig killing, about the hams and the sausages Kula would be selling, and about Christmas. I told them the Russians would soon be in Piasowe. Then the war would be over, and Tania and I would go back to the city. I still didn't want to mention T.; that seemed like revealing too much of our story without need. Warsaw was destroyed; I knew we couldn't go there. I said we would probably live in Cracow. That was where my grandparents were from. I told them grandmother was dead, but we would move in with my grandfather. We would invite them all to visit in the winter, when there wasn't that much work in Piasowe. We would send a horse and cart to take them to G. and train tickets for Cracow. Or perhaps I would come to travel with them so they wouldn't be startled by the railroad and the big city. They shook their heads and said I would be too far away to think of them, but I was excited by the vision of Cracow and being with my grandfather in his house and made more promises: I thought my grandfather would want to come with me from Cracow to Piasowe. Then they would see how strong he was and how he could handle animals. After a day of meeting everyone and wandering through the fields, we would all leave together.

All the while, fear like nausea was rising to my throat. What if the refugee in Bieda wasn't grandfather? Where would we look for him? Would Tania be safe walking to Bieda? What would she do if she was stopped by a German patrol or if some peasant in his cart, seeing her on foot and alone, decided to rob her

instead of letting her ride with him? Never, since
Lwów, had she left me for a whole day or gone so far
away from me. The boys in the pasture liked me, but
they were not my friends. Only Stefa was my friend
here, and perhaps Kulowa, but without Tania I was
like a stray cat that anyone could stone. I decided to
tell them about my father as well: I said I was sure he
would return from the prisoner-of-war camp, in his
officer's uniform, to look for Tania and me as soon as
the Germans left. He was a major; he would be wearing a pistol on his belt and perhaps a sword. The police would have to help in the search. He would not
give up until he found us.

The wind was blowing harder. The cows became
nervous; they stopped grazing and began to low and
move about uneasily. Stefa said that if they were off
their feed it was best to take them back, and that is
what we did. I finished with the cows in the stable,
but Tania still had not returned. Kulowa told me Kula
was asleep; it served him right to be sick after all the
vodka he had drunk; who did he think he was to be in
his feather bed on a weekday? That scoundrel Tadek
had also disappeared, busy vomiting somewhere. She
was making cheese, pouring curdled milk into rectangular linen pouches. The whey had to be squeezed
out carefully into a basin. Then the cheeses, in their
pouches, were arranged on a board, covered by another board with a weight on it, and left to rest. I
helped, holding the pouches for her. We tasted some
of the moist, fresh cheese. We fed the poultry and the
pigs, and I helped Kulowa milk the cows, putting hay
into their mangers so they would keep quiet. Masia
had also disappeared.

We ate the evening meal late, after Kula woke up. By
then Tadek and Masia were also in the kitchen; only

Tania wasn't there. I told Kulowa I didn't know where
she was. The others didn't ask; it seemed to me they
didn't mind being by themselves, with just their little
cowherd keeping his mouth shut except to thank Kulowa for each piece of food. Then it was time for bed;
Masia dragged in her bedding, I brought in Tania's and
mine, Kula said Tania must have found a softer mattress
somewhere else, they snuffed out the lamp, and I was
still alone.

Tania woke me from a deep sleep. She was shivering
from cold and sobbing terribly and kissing me. I kissed
her too and stroked her hair and after a while she told
me what had happened. Getting to Bieda had taken longer than she had expected. She must have walked two-
thirds of the way before a peasant with a cart going in
the right direction caught up with her. He was a quiet
man with a good, fast horse; he refused to take money
from her. When they got to Bieda, he showed her the
house of the peasant who dealt in vodka and drove on.
She had decided to start out by doing a little business
and then casually asking questions about refugees from
Warsaw or elsewhere who might be in the village. This
peasant was very cautious. At first he wouldn't talk
about *bimber* at all, pretending he just sold regular
vodka. He loosened up after she made it clear how well
she knew Nowak, and they drank a glass of *bimber*
together. All the while, she was telling him that she had
many sources of supply and just wanted to know if he
needed more *bimber* than he was getting from Nowak.
He didn't seem very interested, so she said that she
regretted there was no business the two of them could
do, but maybe, while she was in Bieda, she should see
if there were any refugees who had jewelry to sell; she
also dealt in that.

At that, the peasant laughed and said she had come too late, they had had a very fine refugee, with a gold watch and gold rings and money, but the Germans came last week and shot him right against the barn wall. He pointed to his own barn. He was here, that Pan—and the peasant named my grandfather—drinking with me just like you, when they drove up in a big car, four of them with Pan Miska, who has been living in Zielne, over that way. It seems this Pan with gold was a Jew who owned a big farm and two forests. Pan Miska was his estate manager. My Pan was always helping peasants here when a cow or a horse was sick, he knew more about it than a veterinarian, and one day he walked over to Zielne to give a hand with a calf being born. That's where Miska saw him and right away decided this Jew shouldn't live to go back to his estate; better give him to the Germans before the Russians come. Miska told it to the Pan right to his face, before all the peasants standing around in the stable, and my Pan got his hands out of the cow, wiped them on the straw and hit Miska across the face with the stick he always carried with him. Then he spat and said next time Miska wanted to talk to him he should remember to take off his hat first. The peasants were laughing so hard their stomachs hurt, but the Pan went on working with the cow as though nothing had happened. Some of us told the Pan to run away, because Miska wasn't joking, but the Pan wouldn't listen. So they came in the car with Miska, spoke in German, and shot the Pan in the head. Miska is still in Zielne, if you want to see him: he might want to sell the gold he took from the Pan's body. Tania said she asked the peasant for another vodka and then yet another, she was so weak, and then she thanked him; she would see about going to Zielne. After she left him, she walked around Bieda, across the fields, in circles, realizing she had not asked what they had done with grandfather's body but too scared to go back. Then she lay down in a pasture and fell asleep and woke up before she froze, and she wished she hadn't awakened, except for me, because now I only had her left in the world. Night was falling. She began to walk back to Piasowe. She had not eaten and kept stumbling and falling down, and sometimes she wasn't sure that she was on the right road. But she did make it, she kept on saying, more than five hours in the dark, but she made it. We were both crying now and we cried until the Kulas woke up and we had to get ready for work. This was the worst day in our lives.

And so Tania went as usual to see Komar and sell their *bimber*. I took the cows to the pasture. A headache came upon me that kept on throbbing, and although it was again very cold and felt like snow, I was hot and sweating and had to keep unbuttoning my layers of coats to let the air cool my skin. In the evening, Tania felt my head and said I had a big fever. She said my eyes were strange and she could hear a noise in my chest she didn't like. At once she told Kulowa I would have to stay in the house under the feather bed until she was sure I was well; she would pay for having Stefa take out the cows. My fever didn't go down, although Tania made me take aspirin she brought from W., and I remained on my mattress till I lost count of the days, the kitchen turning around me, Kulowa giving me water while I sweated and shook. Tania was sharp with Kula when she came home in the evenings; then she would give him *bimber* and even vodka to make up.

One night she got drunk with him and Tadek; through

my headache, I heard them singing and banging on the table with their glasses to keep time. I kept having strange half dreams; Tania told me it was the fever, she was sure I had pneumonia. There was nothing to do but keep quiet and very warm. On Christmas day, Nowak came with another scarf for Tania and lemon hard candy for me. He was calling her now by her first name only; perhaps saying Pani was too much trouble. The whole family was in the kitchen, eating the ham Kula had kept for the holiday. The smell made me sick. All at once, I heard Tania shouting at Nowak that he must never again touch her arm, never again forget his place, the war was ending and so was her acquaintance with louts like him.

A few days later I was still weak and dizzy but no longer felt hot. Tania came back to the house after the evening meal; she said she had eaten with Komar. When she lay down beside me, she said she did a terrible thing when she insulted Nowak. Komar had just explained to her how Nowak was going to get his revenge. Apparently, Nowak was convinced we were Jews. He had already told the Polish police in W.; it wasn't a question of money because the Polish police didn't want to have anything to do with Jews anymore. Instead they gave the information to the Germans. The Gestapo would come to get us. When she protested to Komar that we weren't Jews at all and that she could show him our papers, Komar asked her not to be stupid, it was all the same to him: he would help us because she was his friend. He would come with his cart and two horses while it was still dark and drive us to the train in Rawa. She trusted him; he even settled his accounts with her. In a moment, she would wake up Kulowa and tell her we were going. She would say there was such a rasping in my lungs that she had to take me to the city to a doctor, even if it meant traveling in this terrible cold.

VII

WE WERE IN KIELCE, WHERE THE FIRST TRAIN WE WERE able to board in Rawa had taken us. The front was approaching. The drumming of the artillery never stopped; Tania said the Russians were only twenty kilometers away. My fever had returned and with it the headache. Tania and everything else around me seemed uncertain and shifting, like pieces of glass in a kaleidoscope, every turn of which brought a new hurt. A doctor came, listened to my lungs, and said the pneumonia was over. Now I had pleurisy; it would probably pass. I should take more aspirin. He was able to sell Tania some.

Once again, we were living in a rented room, in the apartment of a woman who took lodgers. Once again, Tania had found her through the buffet in the station. The apartment was long and brown, our room was brown and greasy; the overhead lamp, useless because there was no electricity, swayed with each wave of shelling. Sometimes a little plaster fell.

In bed Tania lay by my side all dressed. I could not bear to have her under the quilt next to me. I was too hot. We both slept very deeply for short periods. Then I would begin my horrible coughing, and if she did not wake up, I would shake her and ask for milk. But there was no milk left in Kielce. Instead, Tania would heat water with sugar on the little Primus stove and try to get me to drink it, always with more aspirin.

I thought that the bed and my body had grown extraordinarily long. To cool myself, I would stretch my legs on top of the quilt. Far away were my feet. Between the toes I could discern dark bushes crawling with life. Tania put cold, wet cloths on my head. She said these things were as unreal as my old giant; the Russians were before Kielce, in a few days I would be in a clean bed of my own in a large sunny room; she would give me oranges and chocolates. When I wasn't coughing too much, Tania sang to me. There was an old song: Maciek is dead, laid out on a board, but if the music plays he will dance some more. . . . What a polite boy he was. . . . What a pity he couldn't live forever. . . .

Bombs and artillery shells began to fall on Kielce. They were louder than anything we remembered from Warsaw. Late one afternoon, the glass in our windows shattered, and a furious wind began to blow through the room. The landlady came to say everyone was going to the cellar. She did not think we should remain in the room; I could go down wrapped in a feather bed. The cellar would not be colder than the room without windowpanes.

It was like the cellar in Warsaw, only colder and even wetter. A naphtha lamp lit the space and the people inside it, some sitting on crates, some on chairs they brought from their apartments. They all seemed to talk in whispers. The explosions were very near now. There was also the noise of rifles and machine guns. Some of the men went out to look. They said there were soldiers running and shooting at one another in the street; a tank was stopped at the corner, its cannon firing shell after shell. Was it German or Russian? Tania had a bottle of

water. She gave me little sips from it. I fell asleep in
her lap. An enormous explosion awakened me. The cellar was now full of dust, a part of the ceiling had collapsed, someone was shining a flashlight at the cracks
spreading from the hole. The house had been hit. Then
there was another, stronger bang and cries for help. The
door to the cellar had disappeared in a torrent of crumbling bricks. We were buried. The old woman who had
cried out was being helped out from under the stones.
Her head and legs were bleeding. Tania stood up and
said loud enough to be heard over the din that everybody should try to keep calm, she knew how to clean
and bandage wounds. When she finished, and the old
woman was just whimpering quietly, somebody asked,
Why doesn't this Pani lead us in prayer? So Tania began
to sing. She sang the most holy of Polish hymns to the
Virgin. We all sang with her, begging the Mother of
God to bring us a time of goodness.

Late the next day, the guns fell silent. There were
some shovels in the cellar. The men dug a passage to
the outside. We climbed out into a street where other
figures like us were moving about: gray human-sized
insects. It was snowing. We learned we were in a
no-man's-land. The Russians had overrun Kielce, then
the Germans had pushed them back, and now the Germans were gone or were lying low, but the Russians
had not returned. It would all begin again. Tania and
I followed some others from our cellar. They were
looking for shelter in a building two or three stories
high that had not been hit and where they would know
somebody. Finally, they found such a place. After
much beating on the gate, it was opened. Those inside
recognized the people we were with and agreed to let
us come into their cellar. They said that the entrance
was barricaded against the Russians; when Russians

attacked, drunk Tartar battalions were always in the first wave, sent on purpose to kill, torture and rape. We would regret the Germans.

I still had my quilt with me. We settled down on it near a wall. Tania asked for some water. We were handed a bucket; she filled her bottle and began to wash my face. Then, in this dimly lit place, a familiar, kind voice was speaking to us, insistently, calling Tania and me by name. I recognized before us the portly figure of Pani Dumont, a blanket wrapped around her shoulders, a little disheveled, but otherwise unmistakably herself. The cellar was in her family's building; her Belgian passport had saved her in Warsaw from the deportation train; she had managed to get to Kielce. When she had finished kissing Tania and me and we had hugged her to her heart's content, the necessary introductions were performed. Then she fed us, and I finally went to sleep. Hours of bombardment and gunfire followed, the cellar trembled, and once again outside there was silence. Some men went out to reconnoiter: the Russians were everywhere in Kielce; they seemed to be ordinary troops; there were no Asiatic faces in sight.

Pani Dumont, Tania and I came out of the cellar into a blinding January morning. It was no longer snowing. In the street, there were Russian army trucks and armored cars. Soldiers in felt boots lounging near them waved at us cheerfully, offering bread and big lumps of sugar. Pani Dumont was weeping, she said from happiness. All that time in Warsaw she had prayed for us and for Pan Władek, and with God's help, now she knew that at least Tania and I were saved.

VIII

RAZ DWA, RAZ DWA, ONE TWO, ONE TWO, TURN RIGHT, turn left, cross hands with your partner, head high, all wheel, Maciek is dancing the *krakowiak.* He is wearing brown tweed knickers and brown argyle socks, his matching tweed coat has a little belt on the back, in the best postwar fashion. It's all a bit too new and uncomfortable. The tummy has grown bigger and rounder again: with the oranges and the chocolates came sardines and goose-liver sausage and *babka,* the tastiest of Polish cakes—for one pound of flour, one pound of butter. His hands are crossed in the most correct position. They hold the deliciously moist hands of a pink-faced doll with flaxen pigtails, straight from the Cracow *gimnazjum* for girls. The beat is steady, the dancing teacher easy to follow, the accordion first-class.

And is Maciek's name again Maciek? Has the unmentionable Jewish family name been resumed? Certainly not; the visor was not lifted in Kielce; it will not be lifted in Cracow. Maciek has new Aryan papers and a new Polish surname with not a whiff of the Jew in it. Believe me, it is just as well. Tania and he had barely arrived in Cracow, with the plaster of Kielce cellars still in their lungs, the war just ended, when their new neighbors set about holding a pogrom, the first in liberated Poland. Not the old-fashioned kind, to be sure, with aged Jews in black caftans and round hats running around on all fours, youngsters astride their backs, giddy-up horse; you can't find Hasidic Jews anymore. The behavior of our police was first-class: absolutely neutral, hands-off, yet how their fingers must have itched on the truncheon handles! Later in that week some Jews in Polish army uniforms, you wouldn't call them soldiers, pushed and pummeled our boys—pure provocation—on the pretext our Polish boys had beat up Jews rocking and praying at their synagogue. Naturally there was a scuffle, and one or two Jews were sent to rest with Abraham still wearing their shawls. The next day every *żydłak*, every yid in Cracow was in the street parading with a huge sign; utterly shameless. Just like before the war—what do they care if they embarrass the Nation at a time when it needs all the help it can get from the West? Hitler didn't teach them a thing. As for extermination, the Germans could no more get that job done than win the war. They had to leave it to us Poles to clean out the country, as though we had not suffered enough. For instance in Kielce, when the good people there, right behind Pani Dumont's back, finally organized a pogrom—one year after the war ended—they still found more than forty Jews to kill! Can you imagine it?

Tania and Maciek have learned their lesson and do not march to protest pogroms. They have their new names and new lies, except that Tania has gone back to being a maiden aunt. Are these lies still useful? Is anyone taken in? You would not think so. After all, it's true, there are Jews all over Cracow, crawling out from every hole. The worst are the ones just back from Russia, arrived with Russian troops, like lice on their uniforms, only they are again Pan Doctor this and Pan Engineer that, living in the same fancy apartments as before. Other Jews spent the war in comfort too, right among us, eating our food, usurping good Polish names, putting their neighbors in danger, because, of course, we all knew; one could tell those Jews at a glance even if they called themselves Sobieski. And please, how many of them did we keep in a back room for just a pittance, with them always complaining they had nothing left, as if money mattered when you turn into black smoke going up the chimney?

Yes, there are Jews in Cracow again, besides the ones who have returned from Russia: a few like Tania and Maciek who bought their life with a lie and a few who paid to be hidden and were not sold. Some of them have gone back to being called Rosenduft and Rozensztajn and think no one cares. But Tania and Maciek know better: Pan Twardowski and Pani Babińska care very much. These half-forgotten ghosts, with odious names and a look about them that's not quite right, the time will come again and again to put them in their place, even if some people never seem to get it in their heads that they are not wanted. So, the wise Jew's name still ends in "ski" or something like it, even if he isn't fooling anyone who is truly sensitive. Perhaps the ladies with whom Tania has coffee and napoleon pastries in the afternoon are not precisely of Sarmatian stock, but the way they live and their names present a better appearance. They try not to offend.

Maciek's father has returned. He too has a new name, one that fits Maciek's, and lies to go with it; he is learning fast. He has brought home a mistress: this buxom obstetrician, deported from Łódź by the Russians, beguiled his cares in Siberia. He will marry her soon; Maciek is lucky: he will have two mothers. Pani Doctor Olga has a man's sincere grip when she takes one's hand to shake it up and down. According to Tania, it's just as well: Can you imagine her hand being kissed?

The grandparents' apartment has been requisitioned by the new political police; Tania says it's like the refrain of a song; in T. the Gestapo, in Cracow the Bezpieka. A different large apartment with no memories is offered in compensation: the police know who is who. Maciek has his own bedroom again and so does Tania. Pan Doctor and Pani Doctor share the third. Maciek's father attempts an embarrassed explanation; he is offended by Maciek's response. He tells Maciek stories about the Urals and Siberia; Maciek cannot answer questions about the war, however gently his father probes.

Maciek is attending a *gimnazjum*. He has his first real friend. The friend's name is amusing: Kościelny, which in Polish means "sacristan." Together, they serve at Mass, for Maciek is at the head of the religion class and Kościelny is the boy the priest likes the most. Mass is at seven in the morning. Kościelny wants to look after Maciek; he waits for Maciek in front of Maciek's apartment building, since Tania doesn't want him to come upstairs so early and Tania still rules over the household. They walk to church very fast in the morning mist, swinging their leather schoolbags. Picking Maciek up, Kościelny says, is the only way to make sure Maciek will be on time. He doesn't know that Maciek has a will of steel and is always on time and that it just suits him to make Kościelny run halfway across Cracow and stand in the street in the cold. They dress the priest, help him with the holy vessels, swing the censer, ring the bell at the elevation, and wash up afterward. Kościelny's heart yearns for the sacrament; they take Communion. Maciek knows he is again behaving despicably—it is always like the first time in Warsaw—but what is he to do? He cares for Kościelny and needs him and he cannot and will not reveal himself. If Kościelny learns that Maciek is a Jew, he will despise him, especially after the sacrilege, although Maciek is always first in every subject. Yes, Maciek's penis is still his old penis, different from the others, but he has learned that one can avoid urinating in public places or otherwise displaying that telltale member.

Meanwhile, Kościelny cares for him too. Kościelny is tall and very strong. He has tiny ears, deep-set eyes and a small, straight nose with paper-thin nostrils. His father is an assistant railroad station chief, just like Zosia's. Tania teases Maciek about that. Maciek doesn't know how to play games during recreation, but Kościelny excels at them all and picks Maciek for his team. Then it does not matter that Maciek cannot catch the ball or throw it hard or gets winded when he runs. Kościelny is always there and makes it all right. But Maciek declines nouns and conjugates verbs from memory and by instinct, because he knows how they must change, and parses sentences at a glance; these things must be taught to Kościelny with infinite patience, and Maciek teaches him. They take long walks in the park. Kościelny is as chaste as he is strong; when they talk about their bodies, Maciek lies. Kościelny wouldn't understand the truth.

Maciek has a dog. It's a German shepherd that his father obtained from the police school. The dog is barely an adult, perhaps a year old. Maciek thinks they sold the dog to his father because the dog is too stupid for police work. Maciek names him Bari, for one of the stations their new radio is supposed to catch but cannot, because Italy is too far away. Does the dog know that Maciek is afraid of him? They go to the park every afternoon when Maciek returns from the *gimnazjum*. It's late November; the park is empty. Maciek lets the dog run; if he gets enough exercise, he will not be bad

tempered. The dog knows how to come to heel when
Maciek whistles. One afternoon, the dog heels, but instead of wagging his tail and jumping to put his paws
on Maciek's chest to be petted, he is coiled like a spring
and growling. His ears are laid back; he bares his teeth.
Maciek thinks that when the dog leaps he will go for
his throat. Fortunately, the leash he is holding in his
hand is very heavy. When the dog does leap, Maciek
hits him hard, in the face. They continue, leap and
parry, for what seems a long time. The dog becomes
calmer. Maciek turns his back on the dog and slowly
walks away. The dog follows; Maciek hears him in the
rustling of dry leaves. He whistles. The dog obeys, and
Maciek forces himself to put him on the leash.

Some months later, the dog is hit by a car, directly
in front of Maciek's apartment building. An august personage of the new regime lives in the building and there
is always an armed guard inside the entrance gate. Maciek is chatting with the guard, who is his friend. They
see that the dog is dead. Maciek pleads with the guard
to shoot the driver. Tania will later tell her friends at
the café the story of Maciek's grief and broken heart,
that if he could have taken the rifle from the guard anything might have happened. The truth is Maciek is glad
the animal is dead. He tells Kościelny that truth. He
takes the risk that they will stop being friends.

It doesn't matter. One day soon, Tania will leave.
Then Maciek and his father and Pani Doctor Olga will
also go away. He will never see Kościelny again or have
news from him, because Kościelny will not know Maciek's name or what he has become. And where is Maciek now? He became an embarrassment and slowly
died. A man who bears one of the names Maciek used
has replaced him. Is there much of Maciek in that man?
No: Maciek was a child, and our man has no childhood

that he can bear to remember; he has had to invent one. And the old song is a lie. No matter how long or gaily the music plays, Maciek will not rise to dance again. *Nomen et cineres una cum vanitate sepulta.*